BOOK TWO OF THE
PEARCE STATION DUET

Ann Grech

ISBN: 978-0-9954321-8-5
Edited by: Hot Tree Editing
Cover design: Soxational Cover Art

Blurb

Deception tore them apart, but Pete and Scottie are drawn to each other like a moth to the flame. Trust and friendships are tested in Pete's mission to rewrite the legend of the golden reef before time runs out.

Scottie Pearce never planned on falling for anyone, especially not the geeky history graduate nearly half his age. He and his lover have unfinished business. But is nature conspiring against them? The desert trying to tear them apart?

When secrets are revealed, who will be left standing?

Outback Treasure II is a blazing inferno, an epic tale of lust and love. But is time running out as these men fight to keep that which they treasure most... their outback treasure.

Outback Treasure II is a continuation of Pete and Scottie's story. The first book in the Pearce Station duet is Outback Treasure I.

In the last six months Australia has seen some of the worst that nature can throw at us and the fight isn't over. To all our first responders and carers, you are true superheroes.

ACKNOWLEDGEMENTS

These acknowledgements are much the same as in Outback Treasure I. It was supposed to be one story, but Scottie and Pete had a bit more to go through than I could fit in a single novel.

Josh Gates for the initial inspiration, Robyn and Simon Corcoran, Luke Newton and Kaitlin Bryant for your advice on Pearce Station, and everything associated with it and Sharon Hayes for your consideration of the issues around proper representation of our Indigenous Australians. The team at Hot Tree Editing, thank you. Becky, the story is so much better with your eagle eye. And now I can write Ally's story, which I'm so excited about. Your cheerleading abilities are so very appreciated. I'm so glad you adored these boys.

My beautiful friends who make up the MM DreaMMers authors (Viva Gold, LJ Harris, JJ Harper, Angelique Jurd, Tracy McKay, Megs Pritchard, and JP Sayle), thank you for your advice, inspiration, daily pics and keeping me motivated. You ladies are amazing. I'm grateful every day for your friendship.

Tracey Weston from Soxational Cover Art, thank you for your mad skills in bringing Pearce Station to life

Linda Russell from Foreward PR, for your marketing and mentoring, thank you! Your work behind the scenes to get these boys out into the world is truly appreciated.

To my hubby and kiddos, I couldn't do this without your support. I love you all to the moon and back.

Last and most certainly not least, thank you to you, the readers and bloggers, for your unending love and support. Sharing, reviews, general shout outs and, importantly, reading our words means the world to every author. This is my twelfth novel. It's something I never dreamed possible, but you've made that a reality for me. For that – the realization of a childhood dream – I'll forever be grateful.

Ann xx

GLOSSARY

This story is set in outback Queensland, Australia. It uses Australian English. There are some terms that you might not have heard before, so I have set out a few for you. If you come across more, please let me know and I'll try to explain our slang. You might also want to take a peek at my website too – I'll add more there as they come up.

Akubra – a broad brimmed hat.

Autumn – fall.

Ballsed it up – screwed it up.

Barbie – short for barbecue, but in this context it's a grill, not a smoker.

Billy – tea pot.

Biscuits – cookies.

Bloke – man.

Bonza – great, awesome.

Brekkie – breakfast.

Brick shithouse – an outhouse made of bricks (much more upmarket than your standard corrugated iron shitter).

Brissie – Brisbane. Queensland's capital city and location of the Ekka.

Buggered – screwed, broken.

Bundy – Bundaberg Rum.

Bushells – a brand of tea (the drink, not the dinner kind!).

Carnarvon – a town in Western Australia.

Carnarvon Gorge – a national park (bushland) in Queensland, on the east coast of Australia.

Centimetres – metric unit of measurement. One inch equals 2.54 centimetres.

Chips – French fries.

Chook – chicken.

Clip you – hit you.

CSIRO - Commonwealth Scientific and Industrial Research Organization, a government organization responsible for scientific research aimed at improving the performance of industry to enhance economic and social performance for the benefit of the entire country.

Dagwood dogs – a sausage on a stick, dipped in batter and deep fried.

Damper – a form of bread traditionally baked in the embers of an open fire.

Dogger – a hunter of feral dogs and dingo cross breeds.

Drizabone – a jacket designed to be worn by horse riders.

Dunny – toilet.

Ekka – a nickname for Royal Queensland Show originally called Brisbane Exhibition (Ekka is short for exhibition). It is an annual agricultural fair in Queensland.

Fair dinkum – for real, seriously.

Fairy floss – cotton candy.

Fella – bloke, man.

Flannie – a flannel button down shirt.

Footie – rugby league, a full contact sport played between two teams for two forty minute halves where the objective is to score more than the other team by carrying the ball over the 'try line' and, after making a try, kicking the ball between the posts to add an extra two points to the score (called a conversion).

G'day – hello.

Hack it – handle it.

Helluva – hell of a.

Hullabaloo – noise.

IGA – a supermarket chain of independent grocers.

Jam – jelly.

Jocks – underwear.

Jumper – sweater.

Kalgoorlie – a town in southern outback Western Australia.

Kitchen bench – kitchen countertop.

Ks – short for kilometres, a metric unit of measurement. One mile is the equivalent of 1.6 kilometres.

Longreach – a town in outback Queensland.

Lost my shit – become upset or agitated.

Mardi Gras – the Sydney Gay and Lesbian Mardi Gras.

Metre – a metric unit of measurement. One hundred centimetres equals one metre, which is approximately three feet.

Milo – a chocolate powder that you can drink warm or cold in milk, or on ice cream as a dessert.

Mobile phone – cell phone.

Never Never – outback Australia.

Nicked off – left, departed.

Noggin' – head.

Outhouse – an outdoor dunny. Also called a shitter or toilet.

Paddock – a corral for livestock.

Pastoral lease (of Pearce Station) – a long-term lease granted over state-owned land to a person for the agricultural purposes such as agistment and cattle grazing. Where 'exclusive possession' is not a term of the lease (as is the case with Pearce Station), others may traverse the land, such as those who hold permits under the *Mineral Resources Act 1989* (Qld) or the indigenous custodians who have recognized 'native title' rights. Native title was a phrase coined by the High Court of Australia in its historic abolition of *terra nullius* a Latin term forming part of international law at Australia's settlement (the case is *Mabo v Queensland (No 2)* [1992] HCA 23, (1992) 175 CLR 1 (3 June 1992)). *Terra nullius* means 'nobody's land', which justified the importation of British law and customs into Australia, purportedly overriding indigenous custodians' traditions and laws and dispossessing them of the land, and rendering indigenous custodians as 'non-citizens'. The abolition of *terra nullius* by Australia's highest court allowed recognition of the continuing underlying land rights of indigenous Australians where certain conditions were met. Native title allows rights of access, camping or living on areas, visiting and protecting important places, hunting, fishing, gathering from the land, taking of traditional resources (for example water, wood, stone, ocre), conducting social, cultural, religious activities on-site, and the teaching of traditional customs and laws.

Piss weak – pathetic.

PJs – pyjamas.

Pollie – politician.

Poofter – a slur for gay men, equivalent to faggot.

Postie – postal worker.

Prospecting permit – a permit granted under the *Mineral Resources Act 1989* (Qld) which allows for fossicking of minerals, including gold, using handheld implements.

Pulling my leg – joking.

Queenslander – a style of architecture for houses built in Queensland to suit the varied climate in the state (sub-tropical to desert). Traditionally, the houses are constructed on stilts to allow for ventilation and flood waters to pass under the house, with wide verandas and windows all around the house. Painted in a light colour, the combination ensures cooling shade and cross ventilation.

Ranga – red headed person.

Rip-roaring – high in intensity.

Rocky or Rockhampton – a regional city in Queensland.

Roo – kangaroo.

Rubbish – trash.

Sanga – sandwich.

Scoffed – ate.

Scone – a sweet biscuit (i.e. American-style biscuit, not a cookie) that you traditionally eat with jam (i.e. jelly) and whipped cream.

Servo – gas station.

Sheila – woman.

Shit a brick – panicked, freaked out.

Shopping centre – mall.

Sick as dogs – very unwell.

Supermarket – grocery store.

State of Origin – rugby match between the mighty Queensland Maroons (the Cane Toads) and the meh at best New South Wales Blues (the Cockroaches). Usually the Blues have the blues because even though the stubborn bastards will never admit it, Queensland is by far the better team. Go Queenslander!

Station – equivalent to a ranch.

Swag – a canvas sleeping bag.

Tap – faucet.

Tea – depending on the context, either a hot beverage or dinner.

Tele – television.

The Alice or Alice Springs – a town in the Northern Territory, in the heart of central Australia.

Trackies – sweats.

Truckies – truck drivers.

Tucker – food.

Undies – underwear.

Uni – university.

Ute – equivalent to a pickup truck.

Veggie patch – vegetable garden.

Yobbo – a loud and obnoxious Australian, usually a bloke.

Yonder – out there (a non-specific description of somewhere not close).

THE PLAYERS – BYRON'S TIME

Winston Able – the dingo hunter (scalper) who joined the expedition for Byron's gold much later than the others. He was brought in as somewhat of a babysitter when the expedition started to fall apart.

John Blackwood – the expedition leader. He was highly experienced in the outback, having traversed central Australia numerous times on a bicycle and on foot; however, never with a team and certainly not with heavy machinery. He was not a fan of Byron's.

Errol H Byron – the man who alleged to have found a quartz reef in outback Australia laden with gold. He was the subject of Pete's fascination.

Harry Cooper – pilot of the expedition plane, a Gipsy Moth aptly named the *Spirit of Gold*.

Dick Katter – the infamous union boss who funded Byron's expedition by persuading labour union members to invest in it. He was the founder of the Centralian Gold Prospecting Organization (or the CGPO) and ultimately the person who Byron, and Blackwood, had to report to.

PROLOGUE

The cigarette glowed brightly as its owner breathed deep, sucking the last drag of smoke-filled air into their lungs. The window opened in the luxury SUV—a vehicle much more at home on the city streets from where it came than the dusty country road it was on. There was no breeze, but it didn't matter much at that time of year. Spring was a misnomer in the desert. The temperature was either hot or cold. Granted, spring wasn't as hot as summer, but it still hit the mid-thirties every day. Warm days and cool nights. As summer crept nearer, the outback would begin to swelter, the temperature holding at forty-five degrees. Most of the time it was well over fifty—one-twenty-two on the old scale. Asphalt would literally melt in places, and more than one station experienced grain and hay silo fires when the feed heated too much.

The long straight road disappeared on the flat earth in waves of shimmering heat. The landscape was the same as far as the eye could see and many kilometres beyond that. To the unaware, the outback looked desolate. The grey and brown vegetation clung to life, sustained only by what little moisture it could draw in during the brief moments before the morning dew was burnt off by the sun. At that time of day—just after three in the afternoon—not a living creature could be seen from the two-lane road. But the desert was an ecosystem as diverse and complex as any rainforest.

Stark and beautiful. Brutal and not for the faint of heart.

There was no name for the shade of deep blue that painted the sky. It was closest to cobalt, but even that wasn't rich enough a tone. Except for the sun, which seemed a lot closer to the earth in these parts, there was not a single break in the brilliance of the blue. No clouds in any direction. It was probably a good thing too. Clouds meant the possibility of rain, and the few survivors who lived in that region of outback Queensland were tired of hoping. They were battlers, the very definition of the Aussie spirit and they would endure. But it was hard work. Harder than it had ever been before. The red centre was being subjected to the worst drought in recorded history.

There had been no rain in years.

Before the drought had hit, the dry season ended with the onset of the monsoon rains up along the northern coastline of the country, which would slowly work their way west into the semi-tropical zones of the outback, feeding water through the river systems and underground basins as they went. But the last few years had not followed the same pattern. Wild storms lashed the coast. Cyclones had decimated the rich agricultural land and damaged towns to the tune of hundreds of millions of dollars. Flash flooding had swept through low-lying coastal towns and cities causing chaos and destroying invaluable infrastructure. But out west, there was nothing. Nothing other than heat. Temperatures soared and the earth baked. It cracked open, leaving gouges in the vivid red dirt. The vegetation died. So did the animals. The people and their spirit persisted.

Nobody saw the bored SUV's owner flick the cigarette butt out the window. No one witnessed it soar in a high arc and spiral onto the pockmarked asphalt, rolling until it came to rest just off the road against the tinder-dry clump of desert grass. No one witnessed the car speed off into the distance, it's window silently sliding closed as the driver continued their journey into the harsh landscape Scottie Pearce called home.

No living soul saw the spark from the grass ignite and the tiny curl of smoke as it drifted up and dissipated on the shimmering heat.

ONE

Scottie

A nger rolled off me. The others gave me a wide berth. Even the cattle were more compliant than usual. It was as if no one wanted to piss me off more than I already was. My anger was justified. The one time I'd taken something for myself—*someone* for myself—and it blew back in my face so spectacularly that the resulting mushroom cloud could have been seen on the other side of the country. Pete wasn't here for long, but he'd left his mark on me and my memories. The last kiss we'd shared was seared into my mind, playing on repeat. Taunting me. My heart was telling me it was real. His actions, his tenderness, his passion couldn't be faked. Neither could mine. I thought we'd shared a moment. More than one. His fingers in my hair, his body wrapped around mine as we stood there in the cold of the morning breathing each other's air. The look in his eyes. It was affection. Warmth. The beginnings of love? Or maybe it was my reflection I'd seen. A mere dream. The age gap between us should have pulled us both up. It should have made us question how compatible we were, but it didn't make a lick of difference. I'd wanted nothing more than to tell him how hard I'd fallen. How quick. My mind had put the brakes on then, coming to a screeching halt, and I couldn't get the words out. Now it was screaming at me again. Telling me that my heart needed to shut the hell up. The constriction on my chest hadn't eased. The cold hands that had grasped my heart and were squeezing it tight didn't let up. I closed my eyes and blew out a pained breath. Now I was staring at the dirt, wondering where the fuck it all went wrong.

A mining permit. That's what went wrong.

Pete had come to us on false pretences. He'd charmed his way into our lives and in my bed. He'd let me believe a lie. Withholding information from me as important as a mining permit over *my* land, was as good as an outright lie. Now I was faced with a new reality: how could I stop my land from being decimated? How would I stop him from coming in and destroying everything we'd worked so hard to create? Damn it all to hell, he could be sourcing heavy machinery now. For all I knew, he could be planning an open-pit mine. Any effort at grazing sustainably would be futile. Even if it was on a smaller scale than the big mines, water from the Great Artesian Basin would be sucked up and used for wash plants. It'd flow, contaminated and wasted, onto the arid land only to evaporate and drain the millions of years old supply that sustained so many of us out here. He'd walk away with a fortune and we'd be left with nothing. My family would lose our five-generation legacy. Waru and Yindi's sacred sites would be razed. My stockmen would lose their jobs, their homes. The animals would lose their habitat. And for what? The almighty dollar?

No. Bugger that. Not on my watch. This place was mine. It was under my protection. If I had to storm parliament with my whole damn mob of cattle, I would.

I rode Tilly to the gate after surveying the progress we'd made sorting the cattle. I'd called it a night an hour ago, dusk falling upon us quickly. The others had already moved inside to eat, but not Nan. She stood at the gate, holding it open for me as I rode through. She was old now, age catching up with her, but she was still tougher than most of us out here. It wasn't out of the ordinary for her to stand on the sidelines and supervise us sorting the cattle, but I hadn't felt her eyes leave me since she'd walked over to the fence. Dismounting Tilly, I walked her over to the water troughs and slipped off her bridle, letting her feed and water without it in the way.

Exhaustion washed over me, and I leaned up against the weathered timber railing that fenced off the stockyard. I wanted to punch something. To scream and shout. To beat him bloody. But I wanted to make slow love to him just as much. The confusion made my head spin and the headache gnawing at my temple was growing harder to ignore by the minute. I pressed my fingers to the bridge of my nose and breathed out on a sigh.

I felt her warm presence next to me. She didn't say a word, just leaned up against the railing too. When I opened my eyes and looked Nan's way, she pursed her lips and gave me a sympathetic smile. "You right, hon? Want to talk about it?"

"No. Yes. I dunno." I sighed, motioning my hands across the expanse of our land. "I don't know how to fix this. To protect the station."

"We'll figure it out." She was quiet a moment before she added, "I've put a call into the lawyer. We'll know where we stand soon." The fire in her eyes belied the calm in her voice. Nan would do this in a far more politically correct way than me. "Why don't you go and freshen up? Eat your tea?"

"Honestly, I'm not really fit for company." I groaned as I shifted, my tired muscles protesting as I scrubbed my dirty hands over my face. "He betrayed us, Nan. That bloody hurts. I thought he was...." *Different. Special. Mine.* I realized what I'd been about to say a second too late. I'd nearly outed myself without even thinking. Like talking about my sexuality was second nature in this house. Normally everyone was pretty open—you had to be, living out here in isolation; otherwise things would fester—but my secret was one that could never be revealed. It'd destroy everything as quickly as an excavator digging that mine would.

Nan patted my hand, hers frail and weathered compared to my deeply tanned one. But there was strength in hers too and I took comfort in the fact that she was here with me. "Come on," she encouraged. "Or there won't be any apple cobbler left by the time you get in there. You know what that lot is like after a muster."

"Yeah," I grumbled, following her into the house. As soon as I pushed through the door, conversation ceased, and all eyes were on me. Tentative. Concerned. But none of them met my gaze, looking away as I scanned the room. It was probably a good thing too. I couldn't pull off a poker face and I was scared of what they'd see if they looked too closely. My line of sight clashed with the two empty seats that Pete and I had sat in. They'd saved his spot, reserved it next to mine. The empty seat taunted me. Mocked me as much as the memory of our last kiss. I swallowed hard and turned away, pointing down the hallway as I begged my legs to carry me the distance to my bedroom. I couldn't eat with them. That empty seat would haunt me if I did.

White noise buzzed in my ears, drowning out the murmurings of my family gathered around the table. Each step took an effort I barely had the energy for, my muscles protesting the few metres to the door as if I was running a marathon through the soft shifting desert sands. With each step that drew me nearer to the solace of my room, any anger I had been barraged with dissipated. Powerlessness replaced it. Grief poured in. I'd lost him. I hadn't really had him to begin with—a love affair lasting a week wasn't anything most people would write home about, but for me, it was revolutionary. It was something I'd never even dreamed could be a reality. Having him there, know-ing he was with me, that I could reach out and touch him—even if we had to sneak around—was more than I'd ever let myself believe could be possible. And now he was gone. He'd lied to me. He'd put everything and everyone I loved at risk. I should hate him. I did. But I didn't.

When I stepped over the threshold and the quiet snick of the door closing behind me sounded, I didn't find refuge. I was assaulted with memories of him, just like I knew I would be. Curled on my bed with him, his warm body pressed against mine. Our first time to-gether in the shower when he looked after me in a way no other man ever had. I leaned back against the door and my legs gave out from under me, no longer able to carry my own weight. I slid down to the floor and rested my elbows on my knees, dropping my head low. I wanted to cut out the ache in my chest and have life go back to the way it was. But at the same time, I didn't. How could I? He'd shown me what I was miss-ing out on. That maybe, just maybe, someone would like me for me. It wasn't Pete. He was with us for the mining permit, not for me. But maybe someone else would be. I'd given up on finding someone before I'd even experienced what a relationship could be like. I wasn't sure I could go back to getting off a couple of times a year with a random blow job in a nightclub bathroom. I squeezed my eyes closed tightly, begging the grief to wane. Trying desperately to hold onto the last vestiges of my anger. It was easier when I felt betrayed. When I hated him.

I was unsure how long I sat there, but my arse had gone numb, and pins and needles were attacking my toes when the knock sounded on my door. "Scottie," Ally called quietly through the timber separating us. As much as I wanted to be alone, I wouldn't pretend I was asleep. I'd never forgive myself if there was something wrong with the cattle and they needed me. I scooted forward, allowing her to stick her head in and plastered on a fake smile when her concerned eyes landed on mine. Pushing through the door, she held out a bowl with a scoop of the fresh baked apple cobbler and a dollop of cream. "I saved you a bit."

"Ta," I rasped, taking the bowl and placing it gently on the floor to my side. My appetite had fled. I probably should have eaten something, but my stomach flipped uncomfortably when I thought about food. I wouldn't even be having the cobbler that night.

When Ally didn't move, I realized she was waiting on me. I tilted my head towards the bed in invitation for her to sit. Silently, she manoeuvred herself onto the floor, difficult given our rough sleeping and hours travelling. Words I knew she was dying to say were on the tip of her tongue if her furrowed brow and pursed lips were anything to go by. I didn't have to wait long.

"I'm sorry," she whispered.

"It's not your fault he was an arse."

"That's not what I'm talking about." When she didn't add anything, I looked up at her, stopping my fidgeting and waited for her to explain. "I'm sorry you lost him." My heart stopped beating and the air was sucked from my lungs as the room spun. I wasn't sure if it was relief or fear from her comment hitting way too close to the mark. "He seemed like a good man. I'm sorry that he couldn't be who you needed." She looked hard at me, her gaze never breaking mine. I couldn't breathe. Couldn't move. I was like a deer in headlights. Fear crawled up my throat, stealing any hope of speaking. "What are you scared of, Scottie?"

I opened my mouth to answer, but nothing came out. Mute, I had no words to answer her with. I flinched when she reached out for me, wrapping her rough hand gently around my wrist. "I saw the way you watched each other's movements and were in sync. It was as if you'd clicked. Then you gave him up."

"He lied to us." My broken whisper gave away just how much I was hurting. I closed my eyes, this time losing the battle to stop the tears from falling. I swiped at them, not wanting my sister to see me crying, especially over a man, but she reached out, capturing my other hand in hers.

"He did. But I don't think it's as bad as you think it is." She reached for her back pocket, passing me a tattered paperback. "He gave me this. He has a theory—one he's been working on for a while given the state of some of the highlighting. He promised me none of the big guns even have us on their radar. He said he's chasing a myth. I think you need to talk to him, Scottie. Maybe let him explain what brought him out here."

"He wants to mine the land, Ally. Regardless of what he's doing, he wants to dig up our land. He'll destroy it."

"That's just it, he doesn't. He can't. He only had a fossicking permit. I've checked it. I looked at what he can do with it. We do more damage moving the mob around than he can with that permit."

"So what do I do, Ally? Pretend that we're best mates again? Run after him like a fool and bring him back? He'll find a few nuggets and he'll want to get in here with heavy machinery. Then what?"

"I don't know, Scottie." She shook her head, sadness in her eyes.

"He'll sell the rights. He'll get some mining company in here and everything we've worked for—everything—will be gone." The anger in my words had faded to defeat, and I hated that I could predict the outcome so easily.

"When you asked him to leave, he did. He looked at you like you'd kicked his dog, but he left. Waru said that he found him on the driveway just sitting there. He looked devastated."

"Wouldn't you be if you'd lost out on a chance at making millions?"

"At the expense of this place? No. And I think he might feel the same." Ally shifted, using my bed to pull herself up with a groan. "Read the book, Scottie. But when it refers to west of the Alice, picture it being east."

I had no idea what she was talking about, and honestly, I wasn't sure if I wanted to either.

Two

Pete

'd done few things in my life that I was truly ashamed of. I liked to think I was a reasonably good bloke. Until Scottie that was. Now I knew I was an arsehole. I'd wasted the better part of a decade obsessed by a myth. Byron's gold was infamous. Its trail was littered with stories of hardship and failure, of broken homes and ruined lives. I'd fallen straight into its trap, nearly taking Pearce Station and its inhabitants—people who'd opened their arms and welcomed me into their family—down with me. I'd been so focussed, so driven that I hadn't seen what damage I could do. I'd applied for a permit to fossick on their station, their home, and I'd put it at risk of the big mining companies; companies that weren't exactly known for treading lightly on the land or giving a fuck about the locals.

And to top it off, I'd lied about why I was there. The reasons as I saw them were genuine—I was an Australian history major and I did want to connect with the land, but the reason for that connection was far less innocent. I should have told them. I was qualified in extractive mining for God's sake.

Then there was Scottie and me. I could have exposed him. Sleeping with Scottie was not even close to a mistake, but doing it on his property where his family and employees could have found us was. His livelihood depended on him remaining in the closet, and there I was sneaking around with him. I couldn't have been any more irresponsible—not that it was one-sided, but still.

So when I signed the transfer form as S. Pearce, I didn't even feel bad. I stood in the government office three days after I'd left the station, lodged it with the same woman, paid the fee, and immediately headed to the pub. Now I was waiting, for what I didn't know. But I was waiting. Maybe I was letting it sink in—the acknowledgement that nothing would ever be the same again. The realization that my almost decade of research and the tens of thousands of dollars in university debt I had hanging over my head were all for nothing was a hard pill to swallow. I knew I'd reached the end of that chapter and wouldn't be going any further. So, I found myself waiting—for inspiration, for an idea. I had the chance to figure out what to do with my life now. I was starting from scratch. I had nothing tying me down, nowhere I needed to be. No reason to stay. But what did I want? I had no idea. Writing a book was always an option, but sharing my theories and risking Scottie's station further was not. I could get another fossicking licence over a plot somewhere else and take my chances, but I knew I'd always be thinking about Byron's gold and the chance I missed. Not in searching for the gold, but with Scottie.

I sighed, rolling my now empty glass around on the coaster. I was in limbo in every aspect of my life, and for someone who'd had a singular-minded focus for so long, it was disconcerting. The one thing that was certain, though, was that I was leaving this place heavy with regret. The ache in my chest had been a constant companion for days now. My lips still tingled with the memory of his taste, while my fingers remembered the glide of his skin against my own. His warmth, his strength. His affection. I was the idiot who'd fallen for him in a week out on the station under the endless blue sky and on the red sandy plains. It'd taken him days to slip into my heart and own it. I knew forgetting him wouldn't be anywhere near as easy. I wasn't a quitter—my hunt for Byron's gold attested to that—but this felt different. He'd wanted me gone. He'd wanted me off his property and away from his family. I understood that, and as much as it killed me not to drive back out to Pearce Station, I had to respect him.

But I couldn't force myself to leave either. The thought of getting up and walking out of the pub, of checking out of the motel I was staying at, of driving away... I couldn't do it. I'd tried. More than once. Just as much as the man, the desert had ensnared me. Longreach wasn't where I wanted to be, but it was closer than Sydney. The thought of going back to the city, to cars and smog and the throngs of people held no draw for me. I longed for the wide-open spaces of the desert, the red sandy dirt and the blue skies. I longed for faded gold cattle with big horns and a cosy homestead. Most of all, I longed for him.

Scottie

It was the third night in a row that I'd managed to avoid eating tea with the rest of the family. It was obvious I was avoiding everyone. Making myself scarce was in everyone's best interests. I wasn't fit for company. I'd hardly slept, barely eaten, and even looking at me the wrong way set me off. Surprisingly, I hadn't broken a few molars from grinding my teeth together to stop myself from shouting at everyone. It was easier to just leave and manage the station the old-fashioned way—on Tilly. Hours being in the saddle usually calmed me—the wind in my hair and the sun on my face—and connected me with the land, but now all that remained was a desolate emptiness.

I sat on the swing outside of the guest house, Pete's book beside me. Shadows from the moths flitting around the single globe hanging from the rafters danced on my skin, but I barely noticed them. I was lost in my own thoughts after having finished the book. Byron's story was tragic. Overwhelmingly sad for all those he'd left behind—his wife and children. The man was a fraud and a liar. He'd cheated hundreds of people out of money during the Great Depression. Giving them false hope of striking it rich and pulling themselves out of the hell of poverty. Then after swindling money out of the investors, he'd dragged an expedition team around the harshest parts of the Western Australian outback leading into the hottest time of year. For months they'd fought beyond the limits of human endurance for every mile they travelled, in vehicles totally unsuited to the unforgiving terrain and weather. It was a wonder that only Byron had died out there, not everyone. Byron's second wife—who he'd married despite still being married to his first—was long dead, but his kids were still alive. They'd lived carrying their father's unenviable name and reputation. Even as an old man, his son still professed that Byron really had found the reef.

Ally said something about looking east of the Alice rather than west. If the reef was east, it was right around this area. We were almost halfway between Alice Springs and Carnarvon Gorge on virtually the same latitude as Carnarvon in Western Australia. Our gully could easily have been it. Byron's gold-laden reef could be on Pearce Station. I let that sink in for a minute. His reef could be on Pearce Station. I understood why Pete had come here. Objectively it made sense. But it still didn't make me feel any better.

I stared out into the darkness, unable to see beyond the small circle of yellow light created by the globe mounted above me. Trying to get over the man who'd cut my heart out and stomped on it was more difficult than I could have imagined, and absolutely harder than I wanted it to be. Sitting out here probably wasn't the smartest of ideas. Being in the same place as the first night we'd spent together brought back so many memories, but I couldn't exactly avoid areas on my own station—especially when they were places I visited regularly. Closing my eyes, I sighed, resting my elbows on my knees. I dropped my head low, groaning in frustration. The weight of loneliness and loss pressed onto me like an anvil. The uncertainty of my future, and the fear of losing the station to a mining company, swirled around in my belly. But it was nothing compared to the grief I was swathed in. It blanketed me like a shroud, wrapping around me and crushing me.

I'd had him for a week, but the short timeframe didn't matter. The pain of losing him was overwhelming. As if everything was cast in shadow, the world monochrome. All I could envision were long, endless days of aloneness ahead of me. Walking next to my family, but never with them. It was the first time I think I really understood what Ma had experienced when Dad left. When he'd walked away after fourteen years, telling her he no longer wanted to be trapped in hell. It was the first time I understood how he felt too. I loved this place with everything inside me, but for the first time, the isolation was oppressive.

Nan's voice from the darkness beyond the bottom step nearly made me jump out of my skin. "Boy, I've gotta say that of all the times in my life I've been disappointed, this is the worst."

"Oh shit, Nan," I breathed, holding my hand over my heart. "You scared the living bloody daylights outta me." The darkness masked her expression, but as my eyes adjusted, I could see the light grey of her jumper and beanie. She stepped forward, and I saw the disappointment on her features. It was like a punch to the gut. I'd tried so damn hard for so long, carrying the responsibility of this station and everyone's well-being on my shoulders. The money worries, the added pressure of a seemingly endless drought. I knew everyone felt it too, but as the station manager, the buck stopped with me. That meant wearing the burden for Pete's mining licence, but the fact I'd disappointed Nan stung.

I scowled, gritting my teeth together again my emotions see-sawing between defeat and anger that he'd put me in that position. "Sorry to disappoint," I muttered, looking down so she couldn't see how deeply her words cut me. From the corner of my eye, I saw her grasp the railing and climb the steps slowly. She looked frail. She was getting older—all of us were—and in my current mental state, I struggled with that.

"Scottie, I'm not disappointed in you." Her hands were cold as she wrapped them around one of mine, her skin weathered and mottled. When she squeezed, I flicked my gaze to hers and saw tears shining in my grandmother's eyes. "I'm disappointed in myself for not being there for you. I didn't think I was unapproachable, but Ally thinks we might have been. She's worried about you. We all are."

"What are you talking about, Nan?" I questioned, uncertain of what she meant. Unapproachable? Huh?

"I thought you knew that you could come to me. I thought you knew how much I love you."

"I do know that, Nan, but I'm still lost."

"You felt like there was a reason to hide who you wanted—"

"What?" I choked.

"Scottie, we're not blind. Your Ma, Ally, and I, we see you. We see how hurt you are, how much you're struggling. It's not just the risk to the station—we know the extent of it now, and it's manageable. It's the same risk that we've always carried with the possibility of a mining permit being issued. It's the same risk we will always have going forward. This is more. He's broken your heart."

I closed my eyes and shook my head, trying to deny it. But I failed miserably. Tears welled in my eyes, and no matter how hard I tried, this time I couldn't stop them. Nan pulled me into her arms, and I went willingly, crying on her shoulder until my tears dried and I was left exhausted. "Oh Scottie, I wish we hadn't failed you. I wish you didn't feel like you had to hide from us."

"I'm sorry," I whispered, wiping my eyes and trying to sit up, but Nan wouldn't let me get far. She held my biceps and shook me gently.

"Don't ever be sorry for loving someone, Scottie—"

I shook my head. "I don't, Nan—" She raised an eyebrow at me, and I couldn't help but look away. She knew what I hadn't been able to admit out loud.

"At first, I didn't understand the late nights sneaking in and out, and the glances when you didn't think anyone was looking. But now I do. You're in love with that boy and he broke your heart."

"You heard us?" I asked, horrified. My voice was more of a squeak than its usual deeper rumble. Mortification spread through me—my face aflame.

"That's what you focus on?" Nan laughed. "I've been round the block once or twice when it comes to raising kids. I know all the tricks. I did them myself when I was young— except I wasn't sneaking out to meet the station hands for sex. I was smoking and drinking booze." She smiled again and patted my cheek. "I didn't think it'd be you I'd catch out though."

I sobered, the smile falling off my face. "And now, apparently, I'm out for no reason."

"You can be you now, Scottie."

I laughed, but it held no humour. "Yeah, that's great, Nan. I can be me. It's bad enough that now three of you know. Can you imagine what would happen if anyone else found out? I'd be the laughing stock of town, and I'd lose whatever goodwill we've built up with anyone in Longreach. We'll lose every one of our suppliers and customers, and that's after we lose all the hands. All so that I can be myself. Nah, I can't be myself any more today than I could a month ago."

"So, what, you lie down and take it? You live your life miserable and alone because you're worried about possibly losing the hands or your trading partners? What's the point if you can't be happy? That's not the Scottie we raised."

"No, the Scottie you raised"—I pointed my finger at her—"was taught to think about the people important to him. To protect them and do what's best for them." I ran my fingers through my hair and tugged on the ends, frustration eating at me. "There are so many people who rely on me to keep this station running. It's more than their jobs and their investment. It's our home, Nan. If we don't have this, what do we have?"

"You can't live your life as a martyr. I won't let you." Nan's words were quiet but steely in their resolve. "We're all healthy. You could be happy too. All you have to do is be brave enough to go for it. If that boy is the love of your life, Scottie, don't let him go. Chase after him and bring him home."

"Be brave?" I cried, standing up and pacing. Energy pulsed through me. I wanted to scream and shout, the frustration overwhelming me. She was accusing me of being weak, but I'd hidden myself to protect them. Why couldn't she understand that? "Don't you think I have been doing that? Sacrificing myself so that I could be the man everyone expects?" I was almost shouting now, and I hated myself for it.

"This desert, this land will be here long after we're gone, Scottie, regardless of whether this station is successful or not." Nan stood and joined me by the railing, looking out into the black landscape beyond. The weak light from the globe barely pierced the darkness, but it meant I could see the stars lighting the sky alongside the moon. "We have a lot of history here and I'd like to think we have a future here too. But not at the expense of today. Not at your expense." Nan hooked her arm in mine and spoke quietly. Gently. "One day I'll be on my deathbed and do you know what I want to see? I want to see your partner, your husband, holding you. Supporting you." She patted my arm with her free hand, and I closed my eyes at the wistfulness in her tone. "I want to know that my legacy will be happy daughters and happy grandchildren. Please, Scottie, I'm begging you. Be brave for you. Not for this station, not for anyone else. Be brave for you. Fight for you and your happiness."

"I don't even know where to begin looking for him."

"That's an excuse and you know it." I shook my head, smiling at Nan's bluntness. "You have his number—call him. Or better yet, go to the Gateway Motel, next to the pub. He's staying there."

"How do you find this stuff out?" I laughed, hope lighting me up for the first time in days. Maybe even longer, because even though I'd loved every moment with Pete, the need to hide had put a dent in our ability to enjoy each other.

"Eh, gossip. You'd be surprised what you can learn by casually mentioning a certain red-headed boy to one of the good folk from church."

I sighed and rubbed my forehead, unsure of how to feel. "The ladies at church are gonna have plenty to gossip about if they find out. You'll be the poor grandmother of that poofter farmer."

Nan studied me for a moment, her eyes assessing me. Even without looking at her, I could feel her gaze boring into me like she could read my mind if she concentrated hard enough. I resisted the temptation to squirm under her scrutiny. "Do you believe that? That who you love makes any difference to your abilities?"

"No, but everyone else does." I hated the weakness in my voice, but I couldn't mask it if I tried. My biggest fear was the judgement of others stopping me from keeping this station afloat. It took an army of people and contacts to run a station, especially one this size. And if they weren't willing to cooperate, we'd be an island. I couldn't compete with that. I couldn't battle everyone's opinions as well as do my job.

"Who, Scottie?"

"All you have to do is go to church to hear it. Watch the news, check it out online."

"It's a good thing we're not big on caring about anyone's opinions then, isn't it? We've faced adversity before. When your pops died, your ma stood up and demanded to be respected as the manager. There were plenty of people who told her she couldn't do it. Your ma squared her shoulders and walked away. She proved them wrong. You'll do exactly the same thing and we'll stand behind you just like you did with your ma. So will Macca."

"What happens if he leaves, Nan?" It was my second biggest fear—falling in love, then having him walk away. "This place… it's not for everyone."

"Did Macca tell you he wanted to leave? Did he look happy to be going when you ordered him off the property?"

"Of course he wasn't happy. He'd just lost his chance to find gold. I wouldn't be happy either."

"Pull your head outta your arse, Scott Michael Pearce. He didn't tell any of us about it, but he didn't exactly sneak off and go there, did he? He didn't give you any reason to think he stayed here for that. Maybe he got distracted. Maybe he found another priority once he'd met you. Maybe you should call him and talk. Better yet, go and bring him back."

Movement to the side of the house caught my attention. It was Ma and Ally coming to join us, steaming mugs in hand. Ally handed me one as she came to stand on the other side of me, and I gratefully took a sip of the choco-latey Milo drink.

"I need to go into town tomorrow," I said to the ladies gathered around me. "I need to go get him back."

Ally knocked her shoulder into me gently and rested her head on my arm. "Good."

THREE

Pete

I sat at the bar in the pub nursing my first coffee for the morning. I had an eight-hour drive due east to Rockhampton in front of me. After breakfast, I was checking out of the motel and leaving. Longreach would be in my rear-view within the hour, and that thought depressed me more than the hope of getting any relief from the distance I was putting between myself and the man I desperately wanted but could never have.

I hadn't planned any of my journey after Rocky. I figured I'd look around the town, try to get work. Then if I couldn't, it was an easy trip south to Brisbane. I didn't want to go back to Sydney—I didn't even want to go to Brisbane. My short stay in the outback made me yearn for wide-open spaces, big skies, and red dirt. How would I ever return to a city? The traffic, the people, the buildings all crowding around me. Suffocating me. No, that wasn't me anymore. That was B.S.—Before Scottie. There was an A.S. now too— After Scottie—and over the last few days of pondering my future in the glass of whatever I was drinking, I'd come to the realization that the before version of me was as full of B.S. as Byron had been. The A.S. version was a different man. A lost one, but different nevertheless.

The pub was more of a restaurant at this time of morning, but there were a few diehards getting an early start on their drinking. I paid them no attention. I didn't even look up when a man slid onto the bar stool next to me. But I did close my eyes and breathe deep. He smelled just like him, and a hopeless desperation to have Scottie pressed against me one more time spread through me. God, I missed him.

When I opened my eyes, I could feel his on me. From what Scottie had told me about the reasons why he stayed quiet about his sexuality, it didn't take a genius to guess that Longreach wasn't the safest of places to be out. I was… me. I didn't exactly have a rainbow flag tattooed on my forehead, but I didn't actively hide my sexuality either. Combine that with the fact that I looked like a teenaged nerd, and I wasn't filled with confidence in my ability to survive for long in this town. Nerves skittered through me as I looked at the man, hoping I didn't end up with a black eye if he'd caught onto me smelling him. But what I saw floored me.

Shocked me to my core.

I opened my mouth to speak, but nothing came out. Scottie was there. In the flesh, and damn was he a sight for sore eyes. Wearing his trademark hat, a red and black checked flannie and faded black jeans, he looked warm and good and sexy. And tired. He had dark circles under his eyes, and it took everything in me not to reach out and touch him. To make sure he was real and not just an apparition. With nothing but a one-sided tilt of his lips, he asked, "Can we talk? Somewhere private maybe?" I almost swooned at the sound of his voice. My skin flushed hot and cold. My heart thumped harder. He'd rasped that gorgeous voice in my ear when he'd been deep inside me. I'd heard it mumbled as he woke, curled around each other, and sleeping on the hard-packed earth during the muster.

I took a moment to register his words, but when I did, I reacted, pushing aside my half-finished coffee and grabbing hold of his arm, pulling him up. Motioning to the front door, I hurried towards it, stopping only to let Scottie catch up. "I can't believe you're here." I heard the wonder in my voice as we stepped out onto the veranda and down the stairs into the sunshine. The warm desert breeze drifted over me and the conflicting emotions inside me were tumultuous. How could I be both at ease and antsy at once?

"Nan might've told me to pull my head outta my arse." He smirked, and I cocked my head, waiting for him to explain further.

When he didn't elaborate, I pointed to the newish building next door to the old pub and added, "My motel room is just up here." The two buildings sat in complete contrast to one another. The pub was a highset single-storey Queenslander with wide verandas under a corrugated iron roof. The finials and timber fretwork decorating the gables and the underside of the awning were all painted white like the rest of the building. The only other colour visible was the dark timber floors, polished to a high gleam inside. But outside, they were worn and dusty. Dimly lit inside, the rooms were always cool even without air conditioning. It was over a hundred years old and had seen more history than almost any other building in town. The motel, on the other hand, was built a decade ago and boasted light grey walls, tinted windows, and deep red accent walls. I ignored all of it, though, as we cut across the car park and swiped my key card for entry. On the inside, my rust-coloured bedspread and matching couch contrasted against the cream walls and the dark grey vinyl flooring. Scottie was barely inside before I pushed the door closed, trying to give us some privacy.

He was on me then, spinning us around and pushing me up against the timber door with his big body, his hands cupping my face and his knee wedged between my legs. "I'm sorry. I should have given you a chance to expl—"

"No." I ran my thumb down his cheek and resisted the temptation to kiss him. I wasn't sure we were there yet, despite being in each other's arms. "I lied to you by omission. You had every right to react the way you did." I closed my eyes, resting my forehead against his and breathing in his air. He smelled like home. He felt like it too. I was so grateful that my greatest wish had come true. "I never thought I'd see you again." My voice came out as a broken whisper, and I didn't realize there were tears tracking down my cheeks until Scottie leaned forward and kissed them away.

"I was angry at you for not telling me. Then I was angry at you for leaving. I was angriest at myself for sending you away." He let out a breath and his shoulders fell. "Now I don't know how to feel."

"I'm grateful you came. I didn't want to leave, but when you told me to go, I knew I couldn't stick around. I wanted to respect your wishes, but walking away from you was the hardest thing I've ever done. I almost turned around. More than once. But I kept seeing your face, and then Waru came and I figured there was no chance you'd want me back there."

I saw the walls snap back into place as he voiced the words, as if he was steeling himself for my reply. "Was it harder than leaving your fossicking site? Than finding the reef?"

"I've dedicated nearly a decade to rediscovering Byron's gold. I've worked more hours than I can count following every breadcrumb until I found a trail. I turned every stone to get me here." His muscles tensed under my palms and he gritted his teeth together, grinding his jaw. "And yet from the moment I met you, it was like a switch flipped. The reef became completely unimportant. It brought me to you, to Pearce Station, but it's not why I wanted to stay." I leaned in and kissed Scottie softly, just a press of our lips together. A shudder ran through me and I sucked in a breath as Scottie relaxed against me once again. It could have been lightning zapping through me—powerful and all-consuming. I wanted to worship him. To show him exactly how I felt, but this time I needed to convey what was in my heart with words, not by getting off with him. "Your land is everything I never knew I would love. Blue skies and dry, sandy red dirt. It's harsh and beautiful. Wild. The possibility of the reef aside, I love it there. I don't think I'll ever be the same man again after having stayed there." I nudged his nose with mine and traced the shell of his ear with my fingertip, feeling every part of him I could reach. Just touching him.

"You've ruined me for cities. I'll never be impressed by Sydney's lights again when I've seen what a blanket of stars in the night sky looks like." I smiled and breathed him in. "But even the land doesn't hold a candle to you. Meeting you that first day was like a dream and a nightmare all rolled in one. How was I supposed to keep my hands off the most handsome man I'd ever laid eyes on? Even scowling at me, you were more attractive than any man I've ever met. Then we spoke, and you introduced me to Tilly, and I realized there was so much more to you than your looks. I thought I'd won the lotto, found the gold at the end of the rainbow and discovered a whole mine of gems when I found out you're gay. I barely even thought of Byron's reef when I was at the station, but when I was with you? It was only ever in passing. As a reminder of what I still needed to tell you."

"Why didn't you?"

"I don't know." I paused. No, that wasn't right. "I was scared you'd send me away. You have such a big heart and you're such a good man, Scottie. I fell for you so quickly it wasn't funny. I thought you'd tell me to leave. And then you did find out, and exactly that happened. It killed me knowing I'd hurt you."

"I felt like you'd betrayed me. I let you in and showed you a side of myself I'd never revealed to anyone before. I thought you'd faked the whole thing just to get access to the reef. I wanted to punch you, but my heart... well, that stupid fucker wanted me to make love to you. How screwed up is that?" He huffed out a breath and shook his head. "I saw 'permit under the Mining Act' written on the form and

I saw red. I thought you were there to destroy everything we'd worked for. I had these visions of you digging an open-pit mine at the station and eviscerating the land, using up all the water in the Basin. I wanted you gone so you couldn't hurt me or the land."

"I'd never do that, Scottie. Even if I could have, I never would have done it."

"I talked to Ally and she made me see some sense. She explained exactly what you could and couldn't do with the permit and gave me your book. Told me to read it." He breathed in, as if he was psyching himself to say something, and the words rushed out of him. "Even if you did tell us about the reef, I think I would have reacted the same way. I was scared that it was the reason why you wanted to be there."

"I wanted to stay, Scottie. Not for the reef, but for you." Scottie closed his eyes and leaned closer, nuzzling his face against the curve of my throat.

"Will you come home, Pete? You can fossick around the gully. Just, please, don't tear it apart."

"I can't, Scottie." He pulled back and his face fell, flinching when I shook my head to reinforce what I'd said. He tried to pull away, but I held tight, not letting him move. "I transferred my permit. I don't want the rights to it anymore. It's not important. If I come back, it's because of you not because of some remote chance of finding gold. You need to know that. I'm not going to risk you misunderstanding my motives ever again."

"To who?" he asked, his eyes flashing as he pressed his mouth into a thin line.

I smiled. "To you." I cupped his face and ran my thumb over his lips. "I might have kind of forged your signature to transfer it to you."

Surprise lit his features, the frown marring his forehead disappearing as his eyebrows lifted and his eyes widened. When his mouth popped open, I traced his lips again, loving every moment I could touch him. "You meant it, didn't you? You really do want me, don't you? It wasn't just the gold."

"I found a treasure in the outback worth far more to me than gold." The cheesy line hit its mark, and Scottie snorted out a laugh and pressed his still smiling lips to mine.

He sobered and pulled back a touch, before looking me in my eyes. Honesty and affection shone in his. "Come home with me, Pete. I want you to stay."

I couldn't get enough of touching him. Feeling the prickle of his stubble under my fingertips. "Yes, I'll come home. To you."

He kissed me then, long and deep. Our tongues tangled, our hands rediscovering each dip and plane of our bodies. He was so warm. He was love. I tugged at his flannelette shirt, not caring whether I ripped off the buttons, so I could feel his perfectly flawless skin against mine. With the shirt off his shoulders, I growled in frustration when I ran my hands down his chest to his flat belly and touched his singlet rather than that perfect skin. I yanked it out of his worn black jeans and slid my hands under it, practically purring when his stomach muscles contracted against my fingertips. Scottie kissed a trail down my throat, his stubble prickly while his lips were as soft as silk. He nipped me, and I hissed, my hips bucking up against his, his erection grinding against me, mirroring my own.

We stood there, just inside the door of the motel room, making out like horny teenagers and stripping each other until our jeans were around our ankles and the only thing stopping us were our boots. He stood before me, both of us panting as if we'd run a marathon, and I bit down on my lip. I closed my fingers around my hard shaft and stroked. Watching him move, the fiery passion in his eyes as he watched me watch him, had me nearly combusting. "God, you're beautiful," I croaked, stroking again.

He pressed against me once more and joined our mouths, gently this time. I opened to him instantly, loving the slow rasp of his tongue against mine. When he held my hips steady and thrust against me, I barely stifled the moan. It was as if that one move ignited a wildfire. What started out gentle, turned desperate. Heated passion flamed and we rocked and rolled our hips, precum slicking the way. I wanted him inside me. I wanted to be inside him. I wanted to taste him and feed him my cock too, but I couldn't bring myself to pull away from his lips. Scottie pulled me harder against him and controlled our movements, thrusting in a dance that set off fireworks throughout my body. I slammed my head against the door as he moved his lips down my throat, nipping and sucking as he shifted.

I cried out when he pulled his hips back and separated our bodies. I couldn't stand the space between us. It turned into a groan when he wrapped his calloused hand around our cocks and jacked us in unison, twisting as he reached our crowns. The roughness of his palm contrasted with the control he exercised in his touch and had me shooting into orbit, chasing my orgasm. With my fingers in his hair, my other hand on his arse, I spread my legs further and thrust into his grip. He worked us together, his pace only faltering when a shudder passed through me. "Fuck," he growled as he buried his face in the crook of my neck. "There's so much I wanna do to you. I don't even know where to start."

My dick pulsed and my orgasm raced towards me. Unstoppable and fierce, I whined as Scottie closed his hand around my throat, tilted my head at just the right angle, and bit down on my pulse point. The movement of my hips stuttered, and I tightened my grip on him as he rolled his hips one more time. I was a goner. I saw stars. My orgasm barrelled through me, and I shouted out my release as Scottie sucked harder.

It was like an out-of-body experience watching him tilt his head back, the muscles in his throat cording as he shuddered and groaned, his orgasm pumping through his cock in hot spurts. Scottie collapsed forward and I held him close, gentling my grip in his hair. I didn't know what I'd done in a previous life to deserve someone like this man, but I'd take it. Running my fingers through his sweaty hair, I kissed his temple and held him close. Moulded together from head to toe, Scottie chuckled as he felt my cock perk up again when he kissed the spot he'd tortured before.

"You might need a scarf," he mumbled against my skin. Kiss. "Or a beard." Another kiss. "A turtleneck." A soft puff of air against my throat, making me shiver, and another kiss. "Make-up."

"You tryin' to make me look like I'm a seventies porn star?"

"No, just tryin' to cover the mother of all hickeys." He pulled back and looked at me apologetically. "You look like you've gone a round or two with a vampire."

"Nah, I was Team Jacob."

"I have no idea what you just said." He shook his head, a smirk on his kiss-swollen lips.

"Eh, vampire books. Movies. Never mind." I waved my hand dismissively.

My legs were like jelly; it was a good thing he was still holding me up, but when he pulled back, and I swayed, he laughed. "You're like a newborn calf, all wobbly-legged."

"Shut up," I mumbled, making Scottie laugh harder. When he held out his hand, beckoning me to grasp it, I didn't hesitate. I would follow this man anywhere, anytime. He tugged me towards him, and we stumbled backwards, our jeans still around our ankles. When his calves hit the bed, I pushed him gently, and he fell. The grin never left his lips as he reached for the rolled-up towels, swiped himself down with one, and handed me the other. The rest of his clothes disappeared, Scottie kicking them off after pulling out lube sachets and a condom. I couldn't tear my eyes away from his muscles, bunching and flexing as he scooted up the bed and reclined back with an arm behind his head waiting for me. I discarded what was left of my clothes and crawled between his spread legs, dropping a kiss on his hip and belly before moulding our bodies together and leaning down to press my lips to his.

"Do you have to check out today?" he asked. "Or could we spend the day in bed? We can order in."

"Don't know if there's Uber Eats out here," I joked. "And they don't do room service."

"I could eat you." He grinned, wiggling his eyebrows.

"But you don't…" I found myself blushing, not wanting to let him know that I'd thought about it. I loved getting rimmed, but I didn't feel like I was missing out on anything when Scottie held the reins, but I couldn't seem to be able to keep my mouth shut. "Or at least you haven't anyway. I dunno if you do. But that's okay. It's not like—"

"Shh." He pressed his finger to my lips. "I don't normally. It's too personal, especially for a hook-up. But you're different. I told you, there are so many things I wanna do to you that I don't know where to start." I groaned and my hole clenched, and Scottie hummed from below me. He hooked his arm around my neck and brought me down to him, kissing me fiercely. It was all tongues and lips and clashing teeth, and as Scottie rolled me over and climbed between my legs, I gripped his thick arse cheeks and pulled him harder against me.

Scottie was half hard again, his semi pressing deliciously alongside my own as he rutted against me. When he pulled away, I gasped for breath and arched my back, trying not to break contact with him.

Scottie pressed me deeper into the mattress, and I cradled him between my legs as I rubbed my calf against the soft hairs of his leg. My hands on his face, I ran my fingers along his stubble and felt him tremble at my soft touch. The warmth in his eyes, the affection there had me falling into him and pulling him towards me. He came willingly, the gentle touch of his lips against mine stealing my breath. Tenderness in every one of our touches, we kissed and touched until we were both hard and wanting. When he stretched me open, his touches were slow and measured, and I knew what was in his heart without him ever having to speak the words from every lick of his tongue against my opening and glide of his fingers inside me, in every press of my prostate, every time he dipped his tongue into my mouth.

"Scottie," I breathed, arching under his touch. "I'm ready." He felt around looking for the condom he'd tossed, and I stopped him, closing my hand around his forearm. "I want you bare. Come inside me with nothing between us."

He shook his head, nudging my nose with his. "No, Pete. I haven't been tested in a while. I haven't been with anyone unprotected, except for a BJ or two without rubbers, but I won't risk you."

I stared at him, my heart soaring far above the clouds. Then I smiled, and I knew he could see me glowing with happiness. "I think I kinda like you, Scott Pearce."

His grin matched mine when he whispered, "I think I might kinda like you too, Peter McKenzie."

FOUR

Scottie

It was stupid. Four hours was nothing. But I hated that there was any distance between us when we'd just sorted things out. I hadn't intended to take things straight back to his room. I'd planned on talking it out somewhere public so I wouldn't be tempted. But then I saw him sitting at the bar, his head down and looking as miserable as I felt. I knew I'd get the truth if it was just us where no one could overhear. I had faith that he wouldn't censor himself in front of me. Half the day had passed in a blur. It wasn't until our stomachs growled that we'd realized we'd skipped lunch entirely and were well on the way to tea. Pete asked if my offer was still open—for him to come home with me—and after I'd laughed my arse off at him for doubting for even a moment that I'd been serious, we threw the last remaining bits and pieces in his truck, he checked out and was following me home. It was dark, so when he flashed me with his high beams, I knew something was wrong. I pulled up in the drive, about five Ks away from home and hopped out, jogging back to Pete's truck.

"What's up? Everything okay?" I asked as Pete stepped out of his truck, torch in hand.

"This is aroundabout where Waru found me…. I lost my hat."

"What, you gonna look for it now?"

"Figured I'd see if the emu dropped it." His words made no sense. How the hell could an emu get his hat when he was driving? He must have seen my confused look because he elaborated. "I got out of the truck. Went over to the verge over there and I threw my hat down. I was frustrated and in a shitty mood." He shrugged, and I understood exactly how he'd felt in that moment. "Next minute, an emu plucks my hat straight from my feet and takes off."

"The buckle. They like shiny things." He nodded and I grinned. "It was kinda city anyway, City."

He panned his torch over the darkened paddock. "I'm never gonna find it, am I?"

"Nope," I replied, hooking an arm around his waist. "But I've got an old one you can use."

"Thank you," he murmured as he captured my lips with his. I wanted to get lost in him, but I wanted to get us home more. I was about to tell him that we should be going when he asked me the one question I knew would lead to others I didn't know how to answer. "Who knows, Scottie? About us."

"Nan. I didn't tell Ma and Ally, but they know too. I dunno whether they told the others."

"Ally knows about me too. She told me you'd probably kick my arse if you found out I was crushing on you." He was grinning like the cat that got the cream, and it made me smile too, until he asked, "Do you want to tell them?"

I looked away. My reasons for not coming out hadn't changed. There were still the same risks—any one, or all, of my stockmen could walk. Any one of my suppliers in Longreach and customers further afield could say they didn't want to work with Pearce Station anymore and there wouldn't be a damn thing I could do about it. I still had all the responsibility of my family and this station on my shoulders. I still lived in the outback, in a "man's" world. In a place where gay was equated to lesser, to an inability to survive out here. But how could I live in denial of Pete? How could I ask him to hide? It'd be a nail in the coffin for our relationship. If I couldn't even admit to the people around me who I was, what hope was there of ever really being together with him?

"Hey, look at me," he implored, his tone gentle. He waited until I raised my eyes to his. "I'm not here to force you out. I'd never ask that of you. We were doing perfectly fine before, so let's keep doing that. I'm not here to ruin things for you, Scottie."

"It feels like I'm denying you," I admitted on a sigh. "But nothing else has changed and I don't know how to reconcile the two." The defeat in my voice was obvious. It was something I'd agonized over driving into Longreach. Getting Pete back was one thing—and I still couldn't believe how lucky I'd been to find him, for him to have forgiven me being an arse, no matter how justified I thought I was at first. But this was on a whole other scale. I was forcing him back into the closet. Asking him to do something for me that if I got my way would mean he'd never have a "normal" relationship again. We'd never be able to live together, never share a bed other than a few hours of stolen time together in the dead of night. We could never be open about being a couple, not even when we were in Sydney or Brisbane for the shows. There were far too many industry people there, far too many chances to be seen. It wasn't fair to him. It was selfish and self-centred, and I hated asking him to do it, but I was apparently selfish and self-centred enough that I knew I was going to ask him anyway.

"It is what it is, Scottie." He shrugged, his lips pressed into a frown. He was as resigned to the fact that we'd never be out as I was defeated by it. "I know it's not because you can't commit. It's external issues. I get it." He cupped my face in his smooth hands, so unlike my own, and leaned down to kiss me chastely. "We'll work around it. As long as we're solid, I don't care whether anyone knows."

"Will you say that in ten years when we're still sneaking between houses, babe?"

"I don't know," he answered truthfully, and the knowledge that his future might be unhappy broke my heart. I couldn't let the same thing happen to us as what I witnessed my parents go through. Ma's life was lonely, albeit full of people she loved and who loved her. I'd lived the same way before Pete came along and splashed my world in the technicolour hues of the rainbow, but I couldn't imagine going back to it. A few days without him were hell, but a whole future? No chance. That's what the outback—this red dirt that ran through my veins—had done to Ma and Dad. I had to find a way to balance it. To be able to live our lives together.

"But how about we take things one step at a time?" he added.

"Yeah." I smiled. "Baby steps, hey?" When he nodded and motioned in the direction of the homestead, I squeezed him tighter against me. "Let's go home."

Pete swallowed and I could see the nerves playing out in his expression. "I'm a little freaked out, Scottie. What if they're ready to string me up when I get there? Your ma, sister, Nan? Jesus, Waru and Yindi would be totally within their rights, especially if the gully is sacred land."

"We'll face everyone together. I won't let you do this alone and I'll make sure you're safe." The sincerity of my words wasn't exaggerated. I'd string any bastard up by the balls if they hurt Pete, even if it was someone I considered family.

He pressed his lips against mine in a smacking kiss and nodded sharply. "Let's go then." I laughed, appreciating he was preparing himself for what would probably only be Ma sitting at the table. Then again, she was sometimes the hardest person to convince out of all of them. Leading him back to his truck, I held his hand and pressed my lips to his forehead as he sat down.

The drive back only took a few minutes, but even to me, it seemed like a lifetime. I couldn't imagine how much Pete had worked himself up, but it became obvious when he got out of his truck and wiped his hands down his faded jeans. "Shit," he mumbled, wiping his hands again.

"Breathe, babe. Just breathe." I clapped him on the shoulder, wishing I could do more. When he shot me a small smile, I squeezed and nodded in encouragement.

I pushed through the door and froze. Pete crashed into me and we stumbled forward, nearly landing in a pile on the kitchen floor. Ma, Nan, and Ally were gathered round the table, each with cups of tea and a game of Scrabble between them. The conversation ceased and their eyes turned to us as I shuffled in and closed the door gently after Pete came in. Ma crossed her arms and sat back, assessing us. Waiting for me to speak. To own up to whatever I'd done wrong—at least that was what the look was when I was younger. These days it was apparently something else. Words tumbled out of my mouth, and I was inwardly cringing even as I was talking. "Um, hey Ma, Nan, Ally um... Pete's come back to stay. He's got some news about the licence, but that's not urgent. We can speak about it later. He's come back to stay for a while. Longer than he expected. I don't know whether... um... he'll keep working on the station or what he'll do but... um... he's just gonna see how it plays out—"

"Breathe, Scottie. Bloody hell," Ally commented, her eyebrows hiked up high.

"Yeah," I breathed out in a rush. "Yeah, of course."

"Macca," Ma said slowly. "Welcome back."

"Ah, thanks?" he replied, hesitating. It was as if he was waiting for the other shoe to drop. For the interrogation. So was I.

Ma looked around at Nan and Ally, and it was as if they were having a silent conversation. One that I was out of the loop on. Nerves skittered around my body. "If you're gonna be staying here for any length of time, then we should talk about where you're staying. We usually rent out the guest-house. You've paid for it for a few months—" *Oh, shit. They want him out?*

"I'll keep paying for it," Pete supplied quickly.

"That hardly seems fair," Nan added, dismissing the idea with a wave of her hand. "None of our other staff pay for their rooms. Of course, they share with the other hands so maybe we should think about moving you around. We don't have any spare rooms in any of the bunkhouses, but we do have one at Scottie's end of the homestead. It's a little cosy, but if you moved in there, it'd be free. And we could rent out the guesthouse." I was stunned. I couldn't believe what I was hearing. They'd worked it all out. And they'd done it to help keep us together. These women before me were amazing, fierce, beautiful women, and I thanked my lucky stars that they were my family.

"And you wouldn't have to sneak around in the middle of the night. Running between the buildings will get old pretty quick," Ma added, biting back a smirk. They were also smart arses, but you couldn't have everything.

"There's a floorboard that squeaks in the hall. You have to skip it if you swap beds at night. Or you could sleep in Scottie's room and keep the second one for appearances only." Ally shrugged, playing off the gravity of what she'd just said. I could have kissed her. She had no idea what it meant for her to say that. To show her support—for all of them to show it—rather than pretending they didn't know anything about us.

"Ah…." Pete hesitated.

"Well, why don't you show the room to Pete before you decide anything? It's pretty small, but we could convert the storeroom into a bedroom," Nan added. I smiled at Pete and pointed the way. His grin made me smile and his huff of shocked laughter had me brimming with happiness.

"Come on, I'll show it to you." He followed me without hesitation, smiling at me like he was the happiest he'd ever been. Maybe he was. It'd certainly been one of my best days. I didn't bother with the lights as we rounded the corner from the main rooms of the house. The moon always shone through the window at the end of the hallway. I headed past my room and pointed at the main bathroom before dragging him into the room tacked onto the end of the hall. It was more of a storage area, but there was just enough space for a double bed if it was pushed up under the window that ran the length of one wall. The cupboards were the old style chunky solid timber ones from the original homestead. I could always swap them out if he wanted more room. The current sofa bed would have to go to make room for a bed, but I could find somewhere for that without any problem.

"The cupboards have got old papers and stuff in them, but I can clear them out. I've been meaning to go through it anyway. We could store some of our clothes in here—the ones that don't fit in the wardrobe in my room and you could call it yours."

"I love that your family are supporting us, I really do—"

"But?" I asked, ice-cold hands suddenly gripping my heart in a vice.

"I think maybe I'd like to keep sneaking around with you for a while." He grinned and moved into my arms, hovering only a hair's breadth from my lips. "Moving in with each other might be a little fast, Scottie, and I want to keep waking up with you for a long time yet."

"Okay," I mumbled, my disappointment clear as the night sky.

"Don't be upset." He captured his lips with mine, slowly kissing me in the moonlight cast through the large windows. "I kind of like the privacy the guesthouse offers while I explore your body like I want to." He trailed his fingertips down my back and snuck his hands into my jeans, gripping my arse and pressing hard against me. His kiss turned from lazy and sensual to an inferno in a moment, and I bucked into him, wishing he'd move his hands. But he kept his touches teasing, flirting with the desire pumping through me.

When he pulled back, I groaned, frustrated. Resting my forehead against his, I nuzzled his nose and breathed Pete in. "I hate that you're the logical adult here and I just want to jump in head first."

Pete chuckled and squeezed me tighter, but soon became serious. "I love that you can throw caution to the wind and reach for me."

"Let's go tell the matchmakers that we'll wait."

We walked back into the kitchen, and as much as I wanted to be able to hold his hand, I couldn't bring myself to. I wished I could. I wished I could throw off decades of hiding, of being shackled and do something as simple as holding his hand. But I couldn't. Instead, I motioned to the table and asked, "Coffee?" When he nodded and smiled, I moved over to the kitchen to get us sorted.

"Thank you for understanding," Pete said quietly to the ladies in my life. I went and stood at the other end of the table, resting my hands on the chair back while the kettle boiled, keeping my fingers busy so that I didn't reach for him. "It means more to me than you can imagine knowing that Scottie has your support. My parents... well, they're okay with me being gay, but they aren't too happy about the way I live my life. What I've seen here tonight is your unconditional love and acceptance of him." He paused, and I smiled at him, my heart warming at his words. Looking over to me, he smiled too, his eyes full of affection. "When I came here, I kind of blurted out to Scottie that I was gay. I'd intended on keeping it quiet for my stay because I wasn't sure whether you'd kick me off the property. I'm really glad I told him now."

"So, something about yourself you'd intended to keep secret, and you told him, but something you were supposed to disclose to us by law you keep quiet?" I shot a glare to Ally and she raised her eyebrow at me, daring me to back off. Luckily I wasn't scared of my sister.

"That's between Pete and me, don't you think?" My tone was like ice.

"No, it's not," Pete contradicted me, shaking his head. The kettle was whistling so I made my way over and busied myself making the mugs of tea and coffee. I wanted to be angry with Ally, but she had a point, and I couldn't stay shitty with her when she spoke the truth. But Pete and I had already covered this, and his explanation was enough for me. I had hoped it would be enough for them too. But clearly not. Pete continued, undeterred as I made our drinks and watched him out of the corner of my eye. "What do you know about the legend of Byron's gold?" he asked. When Ma shook her head, he smiled softly. It was almost a sad smile. "I found out about it in my first-year history subject, and I got sucked in." He told them all about Byron and his fantastical story of a gold-laden reef whose coordinates were nonsensical.

"Of course they were," Ma interjected, rolling her eyes. "It'd be too easy for it to point to the actual location, wouldn't it." She was looking at Pete like he was crazy. She wasn't the only one. Ally was resting her chin on her hands, her elbows resting on the table looking bored, and Nan was leaning back in her chair with one eyebrow raised, scrutinising him. Pete was holding his own, but he shouldn't have had to. I made my way back to him and placed the mug of coffee in front of him. I wanted to sit sideways on the seat, wrap my arms around him and pull him close, but I didn't dare. I couldn't even bring myself to hold his hand. My heart pounded in my chest as I sat down next to him, keeping a bit of distance between us. I hated it. Hated denying him and hated denying myself, but fear was a powerful motivator. Any one of the others could walk in at any time. Any of them could find out. There were already three people too many who knew my secret. Their support meant the world. It was a relief, like a weight had lifted off my shoulders. I'd stepped into the sunshine and could finally stretch after such a fundamental part of my identity had been stuffed into the back of the dusty cupboard for over half my life. Instead, I turned my head to him and listened, mentally giving Pete the encouragement to go on.

He added, "Byron's gold captured my imagination as a history major. At first, my interest was just as much about Byron as the story, but the more I learnt, the more I disliked the man. What I found though had me convinced that the reef existed. I poured over notes and maps, plotted out journey after journey. Read every piece written about him or by him. I was addicted. Determined to find that reef. I was convinced I could locate it." He blew the steam off the top of his mug and took a sip of his coffee, closing his eyes for a moment as if he was regathering his thoughts.

"But then I realized that even if I did find the reef, I wouldn't know what to look for. What were the markers for gold? How did I extract it aside from running a metal detector over the land? If I was mining, what did I have to do to the payload to get the gold out of it? So, I found out. I buried myself in the library reading every book and article I could find. I spoke to all the extractive geology lecturers picking their brains. I spoke to gold miners, telling them my dream was to go to WA and work the mines. I watched every episode of every gold mining documentary and reality TV program between here and Alaska that I could find. The miners I spoke to all thought I should give it a go. They were convinced I was passionate enough about learning how to do it that I should get out there and try. My university lecturers thought I should do the degree first. They were convinced I'd have a better chance of making it in an industry that was dependent upon brains, but on the face of it undervalued people like me. My parents just wanted me to do something productive—they wanted me to contribute to society. Burying my head in books won out. I enrolled in an extractive geology degree; it seemed like a good idea—"

"You really are a bit of a nerd, aren't you." I smirked and playfully knocked my shoulder into his. I wanted to do so much more, but I busied my hands with my mug. He shrugged and shot me a grin.

"Quite possibly just a little." He huffed out a laugh and continued, "So I struggled my way through the degree and graduated, all the while narrowing down the possible location of the reef. I had a breakthrough and found the gully on Google Earth. It matched. So, I applied for a fossicking permit, bought the equipment I needed, and gave my flatmate notice."

"And you ended up here," Nan surmised. When he nodded, she added, "But you still didn't explain why you didn't tell any of us why you were here."

"The fossicking permit needs to be served on the landowner. I posted a copy of it by registered mail and wrongly assumed it'd take the same length of time to get here as it would be for other places around the country. When I got here, I thought you knew. I figured you'd put two and two together—my name on the Airbnb booking and my name on the permit." Pete hooked his foot around mine and shifted his gaze towards me. I smiled and he sucked in a breath. Flicking his gaze to Ma, Nan, and Ally, he explained, "I'm sorry. I came here thinking I could go camping out at the ridge for a few days at a time until it got too hot out there. I'd thought I could fossick and pull all the nuggets out of the site, then go home and come back next year to get more. Once I had enough to keep me going for a few years, I'd spend that time writing a story about Byron's gold and clear up the mystery. I hadn't thought about what would happen after that—either to my career or to your land."

"And now?" Ma queried.

"And now I know how wrong I was. I pulled up and felt a connection here that I've never experienced before. Byron's gold called me to Pearce Station, but this place feels like its where I'm supposed to stay. Then I met all of you and things changed again. I didn't know how hard it was making a living off this land, and you do it with grace and a soft touch. You have environmental sustainability at your core. You don't waste, you do everything you can to respect the land and the animals on it. You treat it like it's sacred, and it is. I'm ashamed to admit that I'd forgotten that. I got sucked in by the lure of a myth and forgot what was important. Waru and Yindi have their culture ingrained in this land. You have your family legacy. And I had a piece of paper that apparently overrode all of it. But how could it?"

"You *had* a piece of paper? As in past tense?" Ally asked, her pose suddenly alert. Taking another sip of my cooling tea, I let Pete answer her.

"Yeah. I transferred the permit while I was in Longreach." He held up his hand, halting the barrage of questions he as well as I could see coming. "To Scottie. I basically forged his signature and transferred it to him. The transfer is already in the mail; I showed a copy of it to Scottie. I figured you wouldn't want me to hand deliver it to you. But it was important to me that you knew I'd learnt my lesson."

Ally's smirk turned into a grin and Pete's face flamed. "So, to right a wrong, you commit a crime?"

"Well, yeah. But I—"

"Take it easy on him, Ally," I warned from beside Pete. "He did what he thought was right."

"I'm glad you saw how important this place is to us," Nan interjected, throwing a glance between Ally and me. "So, what's the plan now? You still going to go out there?"

"No—"

"Yes," I interrupted, turning to him. "You've spent the better part of eight years chasing this dream. We're going out there. We'll spend a few days camping and fossicking and see how we go. You promised me you wouldn't do any serious damage. I trust you. If you find anything, great. If not, well, you can reassess from there."

"I... thank you." He smiled shyly and reached for my hand, squeezing it before pulling back. I missed the warmth of his long fingers immediately, but I forced myself not to reach for him again.

I jumped when a knock sounded at the door, flinching as Pete's leg brushed my own. He could see me struggling, and the sad smile he shot my way was more upsetting than the fact I needed to hide myself. Jono pushed through without waiting for an invitation to come in—it was normal for everyone to just walk straight in, but Jono always preceded his entry with a knock. He glanced at Ma and nodded, doing the same to Nan and Ally, greeting them with, "Lynn, Ma, Ally". It sounded strange when Jono referred to Ma as Lynn and Nan as Ma, but he was in his sixties—virtually the same age as Ma, so it was what he'd known the entire time he'd lived on the station with us. Then he cocked his head to the side, regarding Pete curiously. "Well, fancy seeing you back here, kid." He looked between us and nodded acknowledging me, "Scottie."

"Come in and take a load off," I offered. When he moved slowly over to where Ma was sitting and slipped onto the long bench seat next to her, I wished that the two of them had married instead of Ma and my dad. "Jono, Pete's here to stay with us for a while. We're going camping at the ridge for a few days so Pete can check out the geology of the area more."

"Sure, boss. Need me to get you set up for tomorrow?"

"Nah, leave the heavy lifting to me."

FIVE

Pete

Jono left after a cuppa, and the five of us remained around the table. When the door closed, I cleared the mugs from the table and rinsed them, trying to shake off the disappointment. I knew everything wouldn't magically be fixed when we got here. Having Scottie's family's support was so much more than I knew he was expecting, but the idea of never touching him in public broke my heart. I wanted him to have what I knew he'd never dared dream—a relationship. And keeping it hidden from the people he was close to meant that he was still hiding. Still living in the shadows as he'd explained it. Then there was his family's involvement. Everything we did would be under their watchful eye. What if we had an argument? Would they intervene? What if they didn't like the way we were moving ahead? God, what if they wanted us to have kids? We hadn't spoken about it, but I wasn't exactly keen on the idea. How did we do this under such close scrutiny? What, if after everything, we didn't work? Or they hated me? Nerves skittered through my veins, and my hands shook when I placed the dry mugs on the bench. I laid out the tea towel on the drying rack and sucked in a deep breath before turning to the table.

"So..." Ally started, "That was a little awkward."

"I'm not ready, Ally. I know you're in a position of having to keep a secret now," Scottie said quietly, then paused. "I know we're family, but Ally, I'm not ready to come out to the whole station."

"Scottie, you're forty years old. You've lived your life in the closet. Don't you wanna step out?" Ally asked, visibly upset. "We want you to be happy. We all do. Why can't you come out? No one's going to think less of you."

"Because there's more at stake here. Do I hate the idea of hiding Pete?" Scottie closed his eyes and ran his fingers through his hair. "Yes, absolutely." He turned to me, and the pain in his eyes took my breath away. I didn't hesitate to stride across the open space and sit close on the bench seat. I didn't touch him, other than pressing my leg against his, winding my foot around his. When he spoke again, he faced me. "But we want to do this right. We want to take our time, get to know each other. Date like normal people— well, as much as we can out here." He glanced around the table and added, "Let us do this at our pace, okay?"

"Of course," his ma responded. "We can't dictate those things for you, Scottie. But you can trust these people. Give them some credit."

✱ ✱ ✱ ✱ ✱

The first twenty-four hours on the station, I spent catching up with everyone and preparing my gear. The cattle trucks had come while I'd been holed up in Longreach, so the beasts that were being sold had already been collected. Those that Scottie was keeping were separated into the two paddocks rested since the last muster. The bulls were farther away from the homestead—an hour's drive across one of them just to get to the gate. Scottie explained that it was inconvenient and expensive on fuel, but it meant that the cattle weren't concentrated in the same paddock they had been in before. Doing that would compact the earth too much under their hardened hooves. Instead, rotating them gave the natural grasses the best chance of regenerating—which of course was minimal given the drought conditions—but the drive to deliver hay and grain out there was something that Scottie was prepared to do if it was best for his land. At least the bores into the Basin were close to the gate, which kept the animals nearby, especially during the hottest months of the year.

The cows, heifers, and yearlings were in a different paddock much closer to the homestead. Feeding them was easier, and being a shorter drive away, Scottie and his hands could keep an eye on them as the cows who'd fallen pregnant progressed through gestation and eventually calving. I smiled, knowing I'd be able to be a part of that—to see new life enter this world and watch them grow. But the picture I had in my head of mumma cow chomping away at lush green grass and the calf suckling would be very different out here. I had no idea what I was in for but sensed it would be a bit more brutal at the station than the rose-coloured view I had of calving season.

We were getting an early start that day, setting off to the ravine first thing so we had a full day out there. Scottie fed the animals close to the homestead just as dawn was lighting the sky, the sun just peeking over the horizon. He jogged over to me, bucket of eggs in hand, as I packed the last of our gear into the back of my ute and pulled down the tonneau cover. "Ready for brekkie?" he asked, standing a little closer than he probably should have been.

"Yeah," I replied, my response breathless. You couldn't blame me. He was looking all kinds of hot in faded jeans, boots, a footie jersey, a blue and white quilted coat over the top, and a woollen beanie pulled down over his chestnut hair. All I could see of his hair were the greying patches at his temples. It reminded me of the greys in his chest hair I'd nuzzled into the night before when he'd walked me back to the guesthouse and come inside to say a proper goodnight. Face flushed from the cold, his breath fogged up the air and his rosy lips made me want to kiss him much the same way I had done last night too. We'd both been left hard and wanting, all because he couldn't stay too long when Ally, Craig, and Sam were sitting by the fire pit outside, but getting a brief taste of his lips had tided me over. Knowing I had him to myself for the next few days was enough.

I nearly missed the flash of heat in his eyes before he darted his gaze around us and stepped forward, caging me against the tray. He didn't say a word, just pressed his nose to my throat and inhaled, his tongue snaking out and licking my pulse point. I groaned, gripping his hips to steady myself and tilted my head back, giving him more room. But it never came. I blinked open my eyes that had fallen closed, and Scottie nudged my jaw closed with his nose. "Soon," he breathed, before stepping away entirely.

I blinked again, adjusted myself, and let out a breath. It sounded as pained as I felt in that moment. "Tell me you bought supplies," I rasped.

Scottie's grinned a one-sided smile. "Yeah, no worries there." He patted the cover on the back of the ute and tilted his head toward the homestead. "C'mon or we'll be late."

I followed him inside, being greeted by a few of the others who I'd seen meander across the yard. It was warm in there. Homely. Fresh baked damper with mountains of eggs and bacon were already served up. Scottie went straight to the kitchen and handed over his collection of eggs before ducking through the door to the hallway leading to his room. I hesitated in the doorway until Ma caught sight of me. "Come on in, Macca. If you need to wash your hands, go for it." She pointed to the same door that Scottie had passed through, "or grab a seat."

I looked down at my hands, which were stained a reddish brown from the dust and grimaced. Holding them up to her, I replied, "Yeah, ah. Gross," and followed the hallway Scottie had taken me down to show me my future bedroom. Reaching the bathroom, I scrubbed the dirt off my hands and walked out just as Scottie was exiting his bedroom sans the jacket and beanie. In black socks, snug-fitting jeans, and his long-sleeved Broncos jersey, the curve of every muscle and that fabulous arse were a feast for my eyes. I trailed my gaze over every inch of him and bless my guy, but he stood perfectly still waiting for me to get my fill. When my eyes met his, the self-satisfied smirk he wore made me want to grab that arse of his and squeeze. Instead, I adjusted myself again and was grateful I was still wearing my coat which covered the bulge tenting my jeans.

Without a word between us, we walked back into the kitchen and Scottie sat down. I hesitated, already feeling hot in my coat. There was no way the now full table would miss my erection if I took it off now and hung it by the door like everyone else had. Instead, I sat down, waited a moment then unzipped the thick material and slipped it off my shoulders, letting it fall to the floor behind me. Scottie sniggered, hiding his smile behind his hand as he rubbed his face and Ally rolled her eyes.

"You excited to do your geek thing, Macca?" Sam asked with a grin.

I smiled at him then huffed out a laugh when Ally elbowed him in the side. "Sam, play nice," Ally responded. "It's his nerd thing."

"Yeah, I am." I paused, ladling a spoonful of scrambled eggs onto my plate. "I can't wait to take a look at the striations in the rocks and see how erosion affects the rock formations out here. It's a completely different world to what I've seen up close before."

Scottie pressed his leg against mine and leaned infinitesimally closer. It was just enough that I'd notice it, but not so obvious that the others sitting around the table would. In that moment, I liked keeping our secret. It was something just the two of us knew—and a few select others—

something private and special. Something warm between us that was growing and taking root that would, one day, be as strong and unshakeable as the old growth trees dotting the station.

The conversation continued and eventually turned to Scottie who started giving out instructions to his stockmen. Feeding, monitoring, and checking over one or two of the heifers who had shown signs of distress the day before. It sounded straightforward, but I knew there would be a whole lot of knowledge under the surface that these men and women had built up over decades of working together.

With breakfast finished, and all of the hands leaving so that they could look after their allotted tasks, Scottie and I ran over everything we needed and double-checked our food and water supplies. We'd opted for canned food for ease of storage, and Ma had packed some instant coffee to go with Scottie's tea. We had the fixings for damper, and Scottie packed some logs for our overnight fires so we could cook and keep ourselves warm. More water than I ever would have thought to carry came with us too. I hadn't realized it, but the twice-daily stops Jono made with us on the muster was to deliver more water. I don't know why it hadn't occurred to me before. I'd always had a tap nearby that I could get water from. Scottie hadn't laughed at me when I questioned whether we needed so much. He understood how sheltered I'd been as a city boy.

After saying our goodbyes to Ma and Nan, we made our way out to the Triton. I offered Scottie the keys, but he shook his head and grinned at me. "Nah, you have at it. I'll navigate for you."

"You sure you want to do that?" I questioned, my brow furrowed. He laughed and went to reach for me but stopped when he seemed to realize what he was doing. Instead, he deflected and turned it into a playful punch to my arm that was so light it barely registered. He winced and I rolled my eyes, letting him know he didn't need to be that careful with me.

I slid into the driver seat and waited for him to get in and point the way. He pulled the door closed after him and sat still for a moment. I was about to prompt him when he blurted, "I don't think this is going to work."

My heart skidded to a halt in my chest, cracking in two. My breath caught as the pain sliced through me. I closed my eyes and gripped the steering wheel, concentrating on the feel of it under my hands than the words that had just gutted me. My voice cracked as I choked out the only word I was capable of, "Oh." That was it. That was all I could say.

I opened my eyes, blinking back the emotion that was more than capable of consuming me whole. The last couple of days we'd been together had reinforced just how much he'd come to mean to me. It didn't matter that we'd only known each other for a week. The idea of living without him in my life, without my being here on this property, sent me into a tailspin. It was as if Scottie and his land grounded me. Gave me a place to call home. But he didn't think it was going to work. Why? Because he'd reached for me?

Scottie turned to me and paled, the colour draining from his face as he took in my obvious distress. "No," he breathed. "No. Oh my God, what...? No." He reached out for me, but I shook his hand away. "Pete, listen to me. Please." I turned to him and let him speak, hoping against all hope I'd misunderstood his implication. "I don't know if pretending we're not together is going to work. It's hard. We might become the worst-kept secret on the station. But I'll get over it, Pete, because not having you is worse than I can imagine. I don't know that I can deny you. I can't lie when I'm falling for you. You're not just my mate. You're more than that. Calling you a mate just doesn't fit. Not with you."

"So... you're saying we're not over?" I asked hesitantly.

"No." He threaded our fingers together and rubbed his thumb over my mine. "We're not over by a long shot."

Relief flooded through me, and I flushed, embarrassed at my reaction. "Might have jumped the gun a little there, hey?"

He pressed his thumb and forefinger together. "Maybe just a little. But I can't blame you. Not with what's happened in the last week fresh in our minds." He squeezed my hand. "I'm sorry."

"Don't be. We're cool." My heart dislodged itself from my throat, and I blew out a breath, relieved I'd jumped to conclusions rather than my fears being realized. That one reassurance from him had all my worries melting away. I moved my hand in an arc. "We need to find a reef."

"That way." Scottie pointed in the opposite direction to the driveway. We travelled through a gate near the homestead and headed west, the rising sun to our backs. Red dirt stretched before us as far as the eye could see, the purple hills in the distance. Tufts of dry grasses and low scrubby bushes dotted the environment, and I closely followed the rough path cut through the desert so I didn't hit anything— wombat burrows could flip the ute, and an echidna's quills would cut the tyres to shreds.

With the windows down, I breathed in the clean air and relaxed into the seat as I drove, watching as the sky shifted from a pale grey-blue to the glorious cobalt found nowhere else but the outback.

I pulled the ute up short and looked at Scottie. Smiled at him. Ninety minutes had passed since we'd left. The homestead was nowhere in sight. We were alone with nothing but red dirt and blue skies surrounding us.

"Out," I ordered playfully. Walking around the bonnet, I met him at his door. Grasping his hand, I tilted my face up to the sky and breathed in. Everything in that moment was perfect. Our entwined hands, the sun shining down on me, the peace and quiet of the outback. The air was still crisp, the day only just beginning in earnest. Scottie moved behind me and wrapped his arms around my waist, his warmth surrounding me. I leaned into his touch, relaxing against him. Just existing. Being in the moment with him. The breeze whispered through the grasses. It was the only sound to reach my ears, except for his contented sigh. Scottie's warm breath skittered over my nape before he kissed me softly and I hummed. Contentment filled me. Happiness right down to my bones. I wanted to get closer to him, to unzip his jacket and climb in there with him. Turning in his arms, I wrapped mine around his shoulders and pressed him gently against the truck, running my nose down his own. Staring into his eyes, I kissed him long and slow until my eyes fluttered closed of their own accord. Then I revelled in being in his arms. Of having his strong body against my own. We stood like that for what could have been a moment or an hour, I wasn't sure, but when he kissed my throat and squeezed me, I knew it was time to move on.

"It's not far," he murmured into my throat. Excitement started to build, but it was tinged with trepidation too. What if after all this time and effort, it wasn't there. What if it was? I swallowed and blew out a nervous breath. He reached down for my hand and entwined our fingers, pulling back so he could look me in the eye. "It's a big ravine. Kilometres long. We might not find anything today or even during this trip. It doesn't mean that it's not the reef, okay?"

He read me like a book. I knew I wore my emotions on my sleeve, but Scottie was observant too. "Thank you." I smiled. "I needed to hear that."

"Always." He lifted my hand to his lips and kissed my knuckles slowly, his heated gaze on mine. "We're not going back early, though, even if we don't find anything." I shook my head and bit down on my lip to stop the moan that wanted to escape. All he had to do was look at me and I was ready, desire wanting to consume me.

He let my hand go and motioned to the ute with a tilt of his head. With his eyes on me, I adjusted my semi and jogged back around the ute, sitting in the driver seat. "Put your seat belt on, Pete," he cautioned in that deep voice of his. A shiver ran through me. Damn, it was hot when he got all safety-conscious on me.

The cloud of dust that had kicked up when I hit the brakes slowly settled, and I surveyed the landscape before me. Towering eucalypts cast shade over the sandy soil. Randomly dotted along the ground were scrubby bushes that were alive, seemingly despite all odds. The ravine in front of me was shallow, but following its path, I could see it deepen and widen out in exactly the same way that I was sure the Grand Canyon looked millions of years earlier. The difference between the two was that no majestic river traversed the bed here. These lands hadn't seen water in years. Everything was tinder dry, the tufts of native grasses long dead, but dense enough that we would have to watch for snakes. The strand of trees ran east, the connection to a forest of old. I didn't know whether Scottie's family cleared their land, or whether it had always been desert with trees following the bed of an ancient creek, but the trees were old. They'd seen centuries of blue skies and red dirt. They'd outlived the longest of lives and would hopefully continue to outlive us all when we were gone and returned to this land.

Scottie opened his door first, smiling softly in encouragement. And I followed. Just like I would always do when it came to him. "Where should we set up camp?" I asked, figuring we'd get the basics underway before we started fossicking. I was expecting Scottie to point to the trees, but he didn't.

"Out in the open over there." He pointed to an area with nothing around it except dirt. "We can have a fire burning over there without the risk of it spreading. How about we look after that in a few hours? We can have a wander around through the ridge first."

I looked over my shoulder at the ravine and smiled. "Yeah. Let's do that."

We pulled some of the gear out of the tray—the metal detector, a plastic trowel, and bucket, just like the ones used by kids on the beach except a lot sturdier, a metal gold pan a little larger than a plate and a backpack filled with water. Scottie pulled his hat out of the truck, and I stalled. Damn, I didn't bring a hat. With my complexion, I'd be burnt to a crisp in minutes without one, even in the middle of winter. I groaned and swore under my breath, making Scottie smile. "Wondered when you'd remember." He chuckled and reached behind the driver seat. The beat-up old hat looked well past its prime. If I was being tactful, I'd say lived-in, but loved. Stained with red dust, the brown suede was brittle in areas, the black stitching around the crown having snapped, leaving a hole in it an inch long. I was a little scared to take it in case the relic fell to pieces. I grinned and bit back a smart-arse remark about it being as old as the hills and Scottie tossed it to me. "Treat her nicely." He winked, and I snorted out a laugh.

"I don't even know where to go with that." I slipped the hat on my head. It fit well enough, a little big, but not so large that it fell off or covered my eyes. It'd certainly do until I could get one of my own.

"You look sexy in my hat," Scottie growled, before closing the gap between us. He pulled out a tube of sunscreen and squirted some on his fingers. "Close your eyes," he instructed, and again, I followed him, doing his bidding and waiting for him to rub the lotion in. His calloused fingers were rough, but his touch was gentle. A caress. Lightheaded, my hands went to his hips to steady myself as he applied the sunblock, covering my face and neck before nipping my earlobe and stepping away.

"My turn," I replied, my voice a rasp that gave away the desire thrumming through my veins. I resisted acting on it. Barely. Instead, I rubbed sunscreen over his face too, and slipped his sunnies back into place.

Scottie cleared his throat. "Right, so um... you want to take a look around first then come back for all this?"

"Lead the way." I grinned and grasped the hand he held out to me. We wandered into the shallow dip in the land, and I immediately noticed the change in surface. "Look at the ground." I pointed out. "Check out how it changes from sandy to rocky here." We continued walking and reached the first of the outcroppings of quartz. The surfaces of some were smooth, as if water had worn away any rough edges, much like a river rock. "Does this flood during the rains?" I asked, wondering how recently water had filled the ravine.

"Before the drought, yeah." Scottie motioned to the hills to the west. "When we had some big rains in the eighties, and again at the break of the drought in the nineties, there was a river that flowed all the way from the range, down along the path of the trees and through the ravine. The one in the nineties lasted for a few weeks, but the pond was there for much longer. I remember coming out here is a kid and going for a swim in the deepest part of it. I thought it was fed from a natural spring, but if it was, it's dried up. The water hasn't been deep enough to swim in for almost fifteen years."

I bent and picked up a smooth piece of quartz crystal, ruddy in colour. "Water has flowed along here regularly at some point, or this wouldn't be as smooth. Quartz tends to be rougher." It wasn't the only rock there. Small pebbles and shards of smoothened crystal littered the shallow dip, as if they'd been deposited here. Another sign of water, another sign of gold. In the US, they were commonly termed desert pavements. The fact that there were extensive signs of a tracer mineral bode well.

"Would the water have washed away any gold if it was here?"

I shook my head. "Gold nuggets are heavy enough that they'll get pushed around but not swept away entirely. The finer gold will be deposited where the water sits—probably your swimming hole—but getting to significant deposits would likely involve excavation to get down to bedrock. Obviously, that's not happening."

We followed the meandering path, and I noticed other changes too, other indicators that spoke to me. The quartz had changed from russet to a purer white. It was possible that the higher acidic mineral solution in the ground had bleached the rock. Colour changes were good. The different types of rock and alterations of the same rock were another sign that gold could be present. It was often found along the seam between the two rocks, or where there was a change in the mineral composition. But I couldn't get my hopes up. There was enough there though—enough clues, enough scientific markers that I needed to swing the metal detector over it. Approach this with more than a curious eye.

"What do you see?" Scottie asked, pausing next to me.

"There are enough indicators here to start detecting. The colour changes, the striations in the rock, and the pavement back where we started." I motioned over my shoulder. "That collection of pebbles where I picked one up is another sign."

"Okay. I can head back and get your gear if you like. You pick where you want to get started."

"Let's do it systematically. Start at the beginning." I kicked at a pebble and watched as it skittered ahead of us, coming to rest against the base of a spindly bush.

"The riverbed goes west too, but it ran shallower there. The water was wider and slower. I don't know if that makes a difference. I brought you to the part where the ravine begins."

"Okay, let's check it out." I smiled at Scottie. Even if I could change anything about what we were doing right at that moment, I wouldn't. Every second was perfect. Being out there in the outback, just the two of us surrounded by Australia in all its glory was perfection. Walking together hand in hand, I savoured the time we were sharing. We'd travelled a rocky path, albeit a short one, to get here. I'd gone through more emotional upheaval in the last few weeks than I had my entire life before. When it was the two of us together, we were rock solid. There were no outside forces trying to butt in and tell us what we had wasn't right. The support of Scottie's family was something I didn't think had even sunk in yet. But more broadly, the wider community's opinions, his workers, his suppliers, and customers were something we couldn't control. I could scoff at the idea that it was not even remotely their business. But it was a reality that Scottie had lived with. Being gay wasn't the way it was done in the outback. It was a "real man's" world. Scottie had more than proven himself, and I hated the possibility that I could unravel that for him. The pressure on him to conform was immense. If it meant keeping him, I'd gladly shoulder some of that responsibility by keeping our relationship between us.

We made our way back to the ute, and Scottie pointed out where the dry riverbed continued in the opposite direction. We stopped and collected the gear I'd brought with us and headed up the riverbed. The red dirt was finer along this spot, sandier. Pebbles were scattered along the surface, smooth as before and mostly the same reddish colour as the quartz at the beginning of the shallow ravine. More of the scrubby bushes had grown below where the foot-deep waterline would have been and the long-dead grass in the area was thicker. Scottie picked up a dead branch from the ground and bent to pick another as I crossed to the other side. Curious about an eroding mound in the land with tree roots snaking from it and diving deep underground, I stepped through the long grass.

Six

Scottie

Pete's gasp had me spinning towards him, excited that he might have already found something. I wanted him to discover gold, I really did. *I think.* But I didn't realize he'd already started detecting.

But I didn't see him holding up a nugget in triumph. Pete had frozen, a look of terror on his face. Before him was a coiled up eastern brown ready to strike. My heart lurched to a halt, panic clawing at my throat.

The snake's golden-brown scales glistened in the sun, its muscles rippling as it hissed. Head lifted and neck flared wide, the snake opened its mouth threateningly. Pete was too close, and it was spitting mad. Sunning itself in the longer grass, Pete must have disturbed its slumber. Given the radiant warmth from the day, it'd be able to move quickly too. I watched in horrified slow motion as Pete let out a panicked whine and stumbled backwards, tripping over his own feet as he tried to back away. The snake tensed, every muscle in its body readying itself for a strike, and then it moved. Pete fell backwards, arms cartwheeling, and a terrified scream ripped from his throat as he realized the reptile's attack was inevitable. It was one of the deadliest snakes in the world, its venom more than poisonous enough to kill a man. And when threatened, they went on the defensive, attacking and striking their victims until they neutralized the threat.

I was too far away from them to help.

All I could do was watch.

Before my eyes, my world unravelled itself. It was like watching an accident—I was powerless to stop it. Knowing the horrors of the next few days and the longer recovery time, if he survived, made the ground beneath my feet shaky. I knew how to treat a snake bite. I knew how to immobilize limbs and slow the venom spreading to the vital organs. To buy his body enough time to get Pete to hospital and the antivenom they stored there. But this was Pete. He could die. And I couldn't let that happen, not when I had a fighting chance at helping him.

Resolve and a whole lot of adrenaline pulsed through me.

The snake sprung, mouth open wide and fangs bared.

Time slowed, and the crash of my heart against my ribcage shocked me.

The snake flew at the man I loved while he fell, his body in motion. I didn't think. I didn't analyse. I reacted purely on instinct. Purely on need. The plastic trowel was heavy in my hand, and I raised it above my head, throwing the nylon-like implement like a ninja star, a roar bursting from me. The hand tool soared through the air, flipping end on end in a low arc. I watched, powerless, as it missed its mark, connecting only with the snake's tail. I ran forward even as the snake was knocked off course, and it was flung to face me.

My actions weren't enough.

The snake connected with Pete's borrowed boot, its fangs sinking into the plastic shin guard he'd strapped atop his shin above the line of his boot.

It pumped a venomous load through its fangs. But it didn't let go. It didn't slither away. It didn't strike out at me. It knew I was there, its eyes locked on me. Adrenaline pumped through my veins as the Eastern Brown poisoned Pete. He'd gone deathly still, his wide-eyed stare focussed on the snake latched to the shield covering his leg as his chest rose and fell rapidly. He was going into shock.

I dropped the bucket as I ran and used the pan like a cricket bat, striking at the snake and sending it flying. It soared through the air and landed with a thud a few metres away, and immediately, I tossed the pan, yanked the shield off his shin, and pulled up his jeans. There was nothing. No puncture wounds, not even a scratch against his skin. I checked his jeans and couldn't find any sign that the snake's fangs had penetrated them. The snake shield bore signs of the bite mark, two tiny holes and liquid—the deadly venom—dripping down the plastic. But it hadn't touched him. "Oh, thank fuck," I breathed. Relief washed over me, and I gathered Pete in my arms, pulling him onto my lap. He was rigid, trembling against me. Eyes wide, he blinked and opened his mouth before closing it again. I cupped his face, brushing my thumbs over his cheeks and rocked us gently. I didn't push for him to say anything. He was still in fight or flight mode. I thanked the spirits and wrapped my arms around him, grateful he wasn't physically harmed. He might not want anything to do with the outback again after his second run-in with a snake in the space of a few weeks.

Slowly, his trembling subsided, and Pete burrowed in, curling himself against me. "You're okay," I murmured softly, stroking my fingers through his hair. His hat had fallen off, but it was the least of my concerns.

"I nearly stood on it. Bugger me, I came so close...." He shook his head and shuddered, then lifted his tear-stained face to mine. "You saved me."

I sucked in a breath and bit back the wobble in my voice before resting my forehead against his. "I was so damn scared." He kissed me then, a soft press of lips against my own.

"You killed it. That's the main thing." My hesitation in agreeing, that split second of doubt in my eyes was enough to have him clutching at my shirt in a death grip and shaking all over again. It wasn't dead. It wasn't coming back anytime soon, but it wasn't dead. Maybe I should have lied, maybe I should have hidden it better, but my emotions were as fried as his no-doubt were.

"Does everything try to kill you out here?" His voice was shrill, panicked. "Maybe I would've been safer staying in Sydney." I knew he didn't mean it, but I wished the thought hadn't even entered his head. As much as I wanted him to stay, I knew there was just as much of a chance that he'd leave, and that thought killed me. Uncertainty and insecurity were a bitch. It wasn't beneath me to play dirty though.

"Funnel web spider, white tail spider. They're just as deadly and prevalent. We have snakes, yes, but you're pretty much right with everything else."

He huffed out a laugh. "Dingoes that eat you? Emus and kangaroos that'll gut you? Fucking snakes!"

"But we also have echidnas and wombats—"

"One'll puncture your car tyres, and the other's burrow will flip it and you'll be dead anyway."

"But they aren't dangerous. And I'm here." My voice held every trace of vulnerability.

"And that's why I'll stay. No matter how many bloody animals try to kill me, I'll still stay."

"Will you?" I asked. "Because I get it. I'd understand if you wanted to leave."

He didn't say anything. Instead, he lifted his hands to my face and brushed his thumb over my bottom lip. When he pulled my hat off and popped it on his head, he grinned, and my heart near on stopped. He was beautiful. Then his mouth was on mine, his tongue pressing into my mouth. He ran his fingers through my hair and nudged my nose with his before he kissed me again, slower this time. He whispered, "I promise you; I'm not going anywhere."

"Good. Then let's find some gold." Pete smiled and slipped off my lap and held out his hand. I grasped it and he pulled me up, wrapping his arms around my waist.

"You're pretty amazing, you know that?" He looked down at me and smiled. "Thank you for literally saving my arse."

"I like that arse." I grinned and squeezed the meaty muscle of said arse. "But you're welcome."

He let me go, and I picked up the shield that had been strapped around his leg, fastening the straps again for him before passing him the metal detector and reaching for my discarded trowel, bucket, and gold pan. He turned it on, checked some of the settings, fiddling with a few things before seemingly being satisfied with it. Then he started the laborious process of detecting over every square inch of the riverbed.

Hours had passed. We'd covered more ground than I expected. Pete didn't mess around, quickly getting into the zone and swinging the gold detector in a slow arc from left to right and back again in straighter lines than I could have imagined. We joked and laughed, then when we'd had enough of the dust in our mouths, we'd stopped for a break. Sitting in the shade cast by the ute, we ate the sangas Ma had packed that morning—roasted beef and corn relish—washing it down with the tea and coffee we'd brought in the thermoses.

"We're still setting up camp out there, aren't we?" Pete asked, motioning over his shoulder to the flat open stretch of red dirt that lay over his shoulder, as we packed up the containers.

My brows furrowed when I saw the nervous look he flicked towards the trees where the longer grass was. Then I realized why. I didn't blame him for being nervous about encountering another snake. I'd never met another person who'd had two run-ins over such a short period of time, both of which were scary in their own right, never mind together. "Yeah, babe. We are." I ran my hand down his spine, stopping at the small of his back and kissed his shoulder. Pete's gasp had me pulling back, worried that I'd hurt him until he pointed west towards the hills in the distance.

"Wow," he breathed, his voice filled with wonder. Only twenty or so metres ahead of us, a mob of roos bounded across the landscape. The big male was a rusty red and was huge, easily my own height. Three smaller roos hopped along with him, their coats a faded grey-red. They could have been females or younger males. I'd seen so many kangaroos in my years on the station that I didn't stop and stare in awe at them anymore, but Pete's excitement was contagious. He had this wide-eyed wonder about him, like a kid in a candy store. His smile was radiant, and when he turned to me, I couldn't help but wrap my arms around him and laugh, happiness coursing through me. "Did you see that? Oh man, that was so bloody cool. Wild kangaroos. I'm… wow."

"Pretty great, hey."

He nodded and kissed me quickly. "I really wanted to see a mob of wild roos."

"I remember the first time I saw one up close. We were about to get in the old Landcruiser Ma had when we were kids. I stepped off the veranda and a few metres away, there was this big red just sitting there eating flowers out of the garden bed that grows round the house. Dad yelled out to me to hurry up, and I said, 'there's a roo here. Someone better get rid of it before Ma goes nuts.'" I shook my head and grinned at the memory. "Dad saw it and freaked out. Bloody hid behind me. Then Ma walked out, took one look at the roo, yelled out for Ally to bring the broom. She chased it away, swinging the thing like a sword. It was a good six-foot-tall and built like a brick shithouse. A big male. Could've gutted her if it kicked out, but she didn't even flinch. Jono saw the whole thing unfold and told everyone while we were sitting round the table that night for tea. Dad sat there, lips pursed and all pissed off because Jono told it how it was—Ma kicked a roo's arse while Dad watched from the sidelines. We ended up eating what was left of Ma's pansies that night just so the roo wouldn't get any more if it came back."

"Your dad didn't really fit in here, did he?" Pete asked, although it wasn't really a question. He knew enough of my parents' story to know that Dad should never have moved here at all.

"Nah, not really." I shook my head and thought back to what we were doing before the roos interrupted us. "Want me to get some firewood together? That way, we can light it as soon as you're ready to finish up for the night."

"Could you?" he asked, relief pained on his features. "That grass…." Pete shook his head.

"Just don't stick your hand in any crevices or try to lift any rocks, okay? And if you need me, just yell."

He nodded and I dropped my arms from around his waist, grasping his hand instead. Pete grinned and kissed me quickly before trotting off to the spot we'd marked so he didn't miss any potential gold-rich dirt.

I hoped he'd yell out, call me with that excitement in his voice, which meant that he'd found something. But it never happened. After I'd collected enough firewood for a couple of nights camping, I headed back down into the ravine and found him standing with hands on hips stretching his neck and rolling his shoulders, the gold detector at his feet.

"Anything?" I asked as I stood next to him.

"Nothing. Not even the slightest blip. I'm wondering whether I'm doing something wrong, but I'm pretty sure I've got everything set up the same as when I got it, and I tested it before we came out."

"Could you have damaged it when you fell?"

"Don't think so. I didn't land on it, but who the hell knows." He kicked at a rock, and it went skittering along the ground, ricocheting off another larger rock. "Thing is, even if it's not Byron's reef, there should be something. The detector is sensitive enough to pick up only a couple of grams of gold, and this is a natural watercourse coming down from hills that are prime goldfields. The indicators are telling me it should be here."

"Could Byron have got it all out?"

He shrugged but shook his head. "This land has been in your family for generations, right?" When I nodded, he asked, "Are there any stories handed down about crazy pilots landing their plane in the middle of nowhere—well, here—and then taking off again? Is there any wreckage?"

"None that I know of, but the only stories I really liked hearing about were the dreamtime stories. It's always been Waru and Yindi who have been the storytellers."

"Can we ask them when we get back?" I nodded and could see the determination in the set of his jaw. Resolve squared his shoulders and gave him a motivational push. "Until then, I'm done for the day. My back feels like I've been through the wringer."

For the next two days, it was much the same. Pete worked, detecting all day, but came up with nothing. Not even a single sound registered. Pete couldn't figure out why it wasn't picking anything up, but I was convinced the damn detector was broken. Perfect, clear nights meant that when Pete had finished for the day, we lit the fire, warmed up the cans of stew before boiling some water and making cuppas. We'd stretch out and watch the sky change from the endless blue into the pinks, purples and oranges of the winter sunset. I'd lived under this sky my whole life, but never truly appreciated it until I saw Pete's wonder. Then when the colours faded and twilight set in, it didn't take long for the stars to start appearing. Their emergence snagged Pete's attention and kept it. We lay for hours in our swag under the blanket of the Milky Way, talking and staring at the sky. Then we'd stare into each other's eyes until we'd go cross-eyed, laugh our arses off and get naked together, warming each other up in as many ways as we could fit in a double swag. It was heaven and paradise all rolled into one. I only wished our time out there wasn't coming to an end.

We'd planned to head back that arvo so we could join the family for Friday night tea. Waru and Yindi were heading home for a week, catching up with their mob before one of their nieces went away to complete an internship in the city. They wouldn't see her much over the next six months, and it was important that they got to send her off. I hadn't said anything to the others about why Pete was there in the first place, but now Waru and Yindi would know. The others would find out soon after. The only other person that might be able to help was Nan. Only a couple of years old, Nan was a toddler during the Great Depression, and I wasn't sure whether she knew much about the history of this place given she'd grown up a few hundred Ks away. But it was worth asking her.

I checked the time and groaned. "S'okay, we've still got a few hours." Pete dropped the rolled swag into the tray of the ute and wrapped his arms around my shoulders. I held him close, breathing him in, nuzzling his throat. We both needed a wash—we were covered in dust and sweaty from three days camping and detecting—but I could still smell that unique scent that lingered on Pete's skin.

"We need to leave in about fifteen to make it back in time for tea."

"I know. But we'll still have a couple of hours where I can hold your hand." He pressed a kiss to my forehead and scraped his teeth along my jaw, making me moan. I was so close to saying "screw it, we're staying," but I knew I couldn't.

So we did exactly what we'd planned. We packed the rest of our gear, did a sweep to make sure we hadn't dropped any rubbish, and made the trip back to the homestead. Pete drove again but didn't let go of my hand other than to change gears. He also frowned the whole way home, his lips only tilting up when he looked towards me. His disappointment was palpable, hanging over him like a persistent fog. The enthusiasm he carried had dimmed over the last couple of days, and I hated not being able to fix things. But searching for gold was so far out of my league that there was no way I could do anything except commiserate with him.

We pulled in to a waiting party. Ma and Nan were sitting on the rocking chairs on the veranda, and Jono leaned against the closest post. He tipped his hat in greeting at us as I eased out of the ute and joined them on the veranda, Pete walking next to me. He wore a smile and seemed genuinely pleased even though I knew he was disappointed. As much as I wanted to grasp his hand, to let him know that I saw his disappointment under the veneer he was presenting, I settled for standing next to him, our shoulders brushing each other's as he recounted our days exploring the ravine, his encounter with the brown snake, and the rock formations he'd seen. Everything except the gold detecting.

But we'd agreed to keep that quiet for the moment. We'd tell a few selected people—Jono, Waru, and Yindi—but not the others just yet. Not until we knew what we were dealing with.

"The erosion wasn't as bad as I expected it to be," he added. "It's clear that fast water flowed through there, but the exposed rock is more likely to have been worn away with wind and sand rather than water. The trees are solid too. The roots go much deeper than I ever imagined. You can really see why you need the vegetation to hold together topsoil."

Jono raised an eyebrow at him. "You went camping for three days to check rock formations and erosion in the outback? What am I missing?"

Pete smiled at me and I nodded the okay to tell him. "We were looking for gold. Just scanning using a metal detector. But unless I totally screwed it up, there's nothing in the section we were in. Not a single flake of it." He huffed and shook his head, finally dropping the façade. I brushed my fingers against his hand in a silent show of support, wishing I could curl my hand around his.

Ma unclipped the chain from around her neck and held it out to him. "Test this. It's gold. It should register."

He waved her off. "It's okay. I'm not worried about it for now. I just want to stand in the shade for a bit, maybe clean up. Feel like I've been baking in a dust bowl for the last couple of days. Even in winter I can find a way to burn."

We stayed around the veranda shooting the breeze for a while, drinking a cuppa until it got close to dinnertime.

The temperature there in the shade dropped and my flannie wasn't enough. "Should we head inside?" I asked, "I'm freezing."

"We should get tea on," Nan responded. "You're up, Scottie. It's barbie night."

"No worries." Pete motioned to the guesthouse, and for the first time in a few days, we parted company. It was a strange feeling, but not all bad. If this relationship was going to last, we needed to spend time apart too or we'd get on each other's nerves. So even though it was strange watching him walk away, I got a move on, getting cleaned up and slipping on a jumper while Jono started the fire burning. The next time I saw Pete, he headed into the kitchen while I tended to the warming grill plate, Jono sticking around with me. We watched the sun set—oranges and purples awash in the sky as it sank to its fiery end for the day. Finally, I couldn't stand the silence anymore. "What is it? What are you thinking?" I asked.

"I understand why you were upset with him now. I thought you were overreacting when you kicked him off the station, but I figured you had your reasons."

"Yeah, I still think I overreacted." I looked down at the rissoles that were cooking before me as shame washed over me. "I wanted to protect us, this land. But I lost my shit with him and shouldn't have. I let my anger get the better of me when I should've just asked him to explain. I jumped to the worst conclusion thinking he was going to mine the site, but that's apparently not what fossicking is."

"Did he tell you when he arrived though?"

"No, he thought the notice would have come in the mail before he got here. It was an honest mistake." I paused, watching as Ally, Craig, and Sam approached. "We're not sharing the reason he's here with everyone just yet. We want to get a better idea of what's out there. So far nothing, but you never know."

"Fair call."

Sam nodded as the trio made their way into the house, and soon after, Craig returned with an extra couple of Bundy ginger beers in his hand.

"There you go, boys," he exclaimed as he handed us the bottles. We clinked drinks and I took a swig, enjoying the cool liquid. "What were you doing out there?" he asked, motioning vaguely in the direction of the gully.

"Pete was checking out the ravine—erosion, rock formations." I flipped the rissoles and added the bacon, listening to it hiss as soon as it hit the burner. "He pointed out some striations which had probably formed millions of years ago. Was pretty interesting actually."

"Sounds... fun."

I shrugged in response, trying not to reveal just how good it was. The fun part was something we couldn't exactly talk about. Well, even if I wasn't in the closet, I still wouldn't tell anyone what we'd gotten up to. There was easily as much sex on our few days away as there was gold detecting.

We ate around the big table inside, after applying all the toppings on our burgers. I settled for good old Aussie—meat, bacon, egg, beetroot, and barbeque sauce. Everyone else did their own thing. Lettuce, tomato, mushroom, and a chip sanga for Nan. We'd grown up with them, but I needed more protein than potato on bread would ever give me. Conversation flowed freely, but I didn't say much. I was enjoying Pete in full-nerd mode, explaining the soil and rock types he'd come across, erosion, evidence of layering over millions of years of history, and the possible places we could drop more bores if we needed them in those paddocks. He'd been detecting and taking all this stuff in while I'd been hanging around playing Solitaire on my phone and carrying the bucket and trowel.

"Waru, Yindi," Pete called out as everyone was leaving, "Can you guys stay for a bit? I wanted to ask you some things about history in the area. I know you're setting off early, so I won't keep you."

"Yeah, no problem," Yindi replied, settling back down.

SEVEN

Pete

Once everyone had left, Waru turned to Scottie. "How can we help, boss?"

He shook his head and motioned to me. "Pete's questions, not mine." All eyes were on me and my mouth was suddenly dry. I didn't want either of them to lose their shit, especially if the land at the ravine was sacred.

"Well, ah…" I hesitated before deciding to just spit it out. "Your tribe has been on the land far longer than any others, but it's more modern history I'm interested in. Have you heard stories about the early plane flights over the land? Maybe of them landing close by?"

"Yeah, we heard stories passed down about the first time the Aunties and Uncles saw them in the sky," Yindi explained, referring to the elders in the way I'd heard her speak of them before. "They were described as birds too big to fly that soared like eagles on the winds. It was QANTAS's early flights from Brisbane to Longreach. It went on for many years. Our people got used to seeing the flights and expected to see planes when they were under the path they took. But they never landed nearby; only when our people were much closer to Longreach did they ever see them land."

"Wasn't there a story about the small bird?" Waru asked. "I always took it as literal—a bird—but maybe it was a plane."

Yindi looked lost in thought and nodded after a time. "You could be right. It was a story about a graceful bird flying low, too low to pull up from the ground. Our people thought it might have been hurt, so they looked for it from the high country, but they never found it. The men hunted around the gully to check whether they could see anything. The river wasn't yet flowing—the wet season hadn't hit—but the storms were brewing. The clouds rolled in the sky and the rains were days away. When the rains came, the river would flow and there'd be good tucker there. The animals would come to drink, and the men would lay in wait for them. But an injured bird could be in pain. It could die slowly, and they didn't wish that. It could draw the predators too. The men went early. They walked for days and camped at night. When they arrived at Allyra, they saw the bird taking off. Beautiful and white it soared. They watched it until it disappeared. The land had healed it."

"What do you mean 'at Allyra'? Is that the name of the ravine?" I asked, my mind going a mile a minute. QANTAS, the Australian-born airline started operating in the 1920s. "Years passing" wasn't exactly a certain enough measure that I could tie Byron to the location, but it wasn't too far a leap to interpret Yindi's story as being a plane landing, with it taking off a few days later.

"Yes," Waru answered this time. "Why? What's important about it?"

"First, one other question—is the ravine sacred ground to you?"

"Not ceremonial, no. But sacred in that it sustained our mob for many years. The wet seasons would always see us return to these areas so that we could hunt."

Scottie looked at me and I let out a breath. "Okay. So, you saw the planes flying along the flight paths for years. Then you saw a bird, possibly a smaller plane, land near… what did you call it? Allyra?"

"Yes, quartz. Allyra."

I pondered that for a moment. Then it hit me. "Wait up? Isn't Ally's name Allyra?"

"Yeah," Scottie responded. "Pop's friend, one of the Uncles, told Ma the translation, and she loved the connection to the land."

"Is this the only Allyra around? As in the ravine, not Ally."

"There are some smaller areas downstream where there is a lot of quartz in the riverbed, but not as much as at Allyra."

"Okay, let me get this straight," I mused. "Assuming it was a plane, not a bird, it landed somewhere near Allyra. The occupants stayed for a few nights and then they left again. The ravine is known by your peoples," I motioned to Yindi and Waru, "as Allyra, and quartz is a known indicator of gold. It's also the most populace rock on earth, so that alone isn't a guarantee, but it fits Byron's story. I can't accurately gauge the timeline, so it might not have been him, and it might not have even been a plane that your peoples were talking about, but stranger things have happened." I paused, thinking things through. Thinking about the flights Byron and Cooper would have made. "I wonder if they needed to refuel," I said, voicing my thoughts. "They wouldn't have wanted to draw attention to themselves by going into Longreach, especially if they had gold on board."

"Nan," Scottie called out, waiting until she popped her head through the door. "Did Pop or maybe Grandpa ever talk about strangers coming by on foot asking for airplane fuel? Would have been around the time of the Great Depression."

Nan shook her head. "Can't say they did, no. Why's that? Something about the ravine?"

"Yeah, we're piecing together stories, and Pete thinks that Byron might have landed nearby, but the stories don't exactly make it clear, and there are some pretty large time gaps that we're trying to narrow down. And in any event, there was no gold where we looked. Either Byron took it all, which seems unlikely if he was only there for a short period and didn't have the kind of technology that Pete was using, or the tech is screwed."

"I think the tech is screwed," I muttered. "What else could it be?" He scratched his head and sighed.

"So walk through it. Let's piece it together," Scottie encouraged.

"Okay." I nodded thoughtfully. "Byron tricked the Centralian Gold Prospecting Organisation into setting him up with equipment and men to mine a quartz reef in the outback. I think he dropped a reference to Carnarvon by accident, and in doing so, revealed far more than he'd ever intended. When everyone assumed it was Carnarvon in WA, he didn't disagree. Historical records confirm he told everyone it was west of the Alice, and there is no doubt that the expedition took off on a wild goose chase. The expedition leader, Blackwood, wrote a diary. It confirmed that Byron and Cooper, the pilot, were tight. When Cooper got injured and went to Alice Springs for treatment, there are records of correspondence with the CGPO that he was insisting on the need for another plane, against Blackwood's advice. When one was delivered and he was ready to fly out, Cooper received news that Blackwood had disbanded the expedition and sent Byron with the dingo scalper on a couple of horses to see if they could find the reef. A few weeks later, Able, the scalper, shows up at the Alice saying that he and Bryon had had a falling out, and Byron went off on his own. Cooper apparently went in search of Byron, but it's unclear whether this was before or after Able arrived in Alice Springs. There is no evidence of where Cooper went. He just disappeared until his plane is seen around Uluru. Able said that they were a few hundred miles away from Uluru when they parted company, but would Byron have travelled there without it being pre-arranged? The tourist trade wasn't exactly thriving at the rock during the Great Depression, so it's not like he could catch a Greyhound bus back into Alice. After that, there's nothing written about either one of them until Byron's body supposedly shows up in the desert. The trail literally goes cold. Cooper's plane could have made Alice Springs to Uluru, then again to Allyra if they had a fuel drop somewhere. Cooper could have organized that himself or paid someone to do it for him. Now we know that Yindi's people could have seen a plane land near Allyra. The timeframe is uncertain, except that it was years after QANTAS started flying between Brisbane and Longreach. The bird was low in the sky, the men went looking for it, but when they got close, the bird took off again and soared away, never to be heard of again. If it was a plane, we could get historical records of flights, but getting them from small airstrips is a pain in the arse, assuming the records go back that far. *If* they even kept records. Rocky airport was opened in 1930, but there were tons of smaller airstrips surrounding it that they would have been more likely to have landed at, and that's assuming they went due east. Depending on how much fuel they had, they could have gone further afield. If they were leaving the country, Darwin, Brisbane, or Sydney would have been the best places to catch a ship from, but they could easily have changed their identities and stayed in the area."

Scottie ran his hands through his hair and hummed, his contemplation of my verbal diarrhoea obvious. "Where to from here?" he asked.

"I wish I knew." I sighed, groaning in frustration. It wasn't the first time I'd taken one step forward, only to take three steps back. "Maybe back to the ravine after I've had the detector checked, but if it's damaged, it might need to be sent away for repairs. Worst case it won't be able to be fixed and I'll need a new one. But, frankly, I'm broke." I could almost taste it. I knew I was close, closer than anyone had been since Byron. But that hurdle—the one which involved me paying for repairs on a detector that might be better off in the scrapheap with my non-existent cash— might not be able to be overcome.

"I owe you some cash." Scottie gently knocked his shoulder into mine.

"What for? I'm not accepting your charity, Scottie." I flashed him an unimpressed look. There was no way I'd start down that road. It was bad enough I was going to run out of money with no employment prospects, but the thought of borrowing from Scottie and dragging him and his family along a path that had more twists and turns than a rollercoaster was not something I was prepared to do.

"No, seriously, you helped on the muster. I owe you for the few days' work you put in. I'm guessing it'd be enough to get the detector at least looked at." Scottie's eyes were warm, encouraging. I knew he wanted me to accept his help. It was obvious, but he'd never have given me a job if it weren't for us sleeping together. He didn't need an extra body on the muster, and he'd spent just as much time babysitting me at the ravine as I'd spent tagging along on the muster. Whatever I earned in wages, I'd have to pay him for the same.

"Let's talk about it later," I muttered, trying to placate him.

"Okay," he replied simply, in that authoritative tone that he used with his staff. "Let's do that."

Waru sat back and crossed his arms over his chest, his brow furrowed. He looked pissed. "That's why the boss kicked you off the property, wasn't it?" he asked, accusation in his tone. "That's why you were upset? Because Scottie wouldn't let you look for any gold."

"Not quite," I answered. "I didn't tell Scottie why I was here. I kind of got sidetracked and…." I pursed my lips together, and blew out a breath, willing my voice not to wobble. "I should have told him, but I didn't. Then he found out and rightfully wanted me to go."

"So, what's different now?" Yindi asked, raising an eyebrow. When she turned to Scottie, her gaze hard, I was glad for Scottie hooking his foot around mine. I didn't even realize I'd clenched my fists and was white knuckling the lone fork left on the table until he shifted closer, pressing his thigh against mine and rubbing his socked toes against the arch of my foot. "You changed your mind, Scottie? You gonna let him dig up the land?"

"No," Scottie and I both responded at the same time. I couldn't help it, but when Scottie tapped my foot with his, I stopped, letting him have his say. "I overreacted. The permit Pete has doesn't allow him to do anything except use hand tools to fossick. He's not going to destroy the land. I promise you I would never have let that happen." His words were quiet, but they were filled with steel. Even if I didn't know it before, his promise left me in no doubt that he'd defend his land with everything in his being.

"I transferred the permit to Scottie. He has complete control of whether we even go out there or not, and if we go out, how we search for it. But I need you to understand that I didn't come back here for the gold. I came back because I want to be here, more than anywhere else in the world. This place... it feels like home."

They looked me over, Yindi's gaze never breaking mine. She was studying me, assessing me. I just hoped I passed muster. Eventually Yindi nodded and said, "I believe you." She smiled. "I knew there was something different about you."

We bid Waru and Yindi goodnight and, after making a cuppa, sat in the loungeroom with Nan and Ma to watch an old action movie. It wasn't a hardship joining them—I'd had a crush on Ben Affleck for years, except I preferred the older version of the man I'd fantasized over than the one that was drilling on an asteroid out in space.

The only seats free were the three-seater lounge, so when Scottie sat at one end, I automatically went to the other. It didn't take long for him to nudge me and tilt his head, motioning me to move closer to him. I shuffled along the couch, eliminating the distance between us until I was leaning on his broad chest. He smelt so damn good, and I snuggled into him watching my crush achieve the unachievable and save the world. Except that I didn't see any of the last thirty minutes or so of the movie, or the beginning of the next one. Warm and comfortable, I fell asleep in his arms. It wasn't until I heard voices and laughing that I woke up to a seemingly nonchalant Scottie—except for his heart almost beating out of his chest—and Sam and Craig having a go at him for cuddling me. Ally didn't look impressed, shushing both the brothers when they continued to tease Scottie. It took a moment for me to fully register what was going on, but when he spoke, it was like a dagger piercing my heart. "Mate, I'm secure enough in my sexuality to have a bloke fall asleep on me without being worried I'll like it."

"He follows you round like a bloody pup. Then he falls asleep on you. Mate, you never know what these city types are like. Who they sleep with," Craig, the most arseholish of the brothers quipped.

"Don't be a shit, Craig," Ally warned.

"Sorry, Scottie," I mumbled, ignoring the others while I shifted off him and rubbed my eyes. "I fell asleep."

"You did." He chuckled. "But it's okay."

"Yeah, I heard. Good thing you're secure enough not to misunderstand my falling asleep as coming onto you." The bite in my retort was harsher than I intended, but I couldn't help it. It hurt hearing Scottie not only deflect but outright lie about our relationship. I knew it was what I'd signed up for, what I'd have to get used to. I just hoped it'd get easier hearing his dismissal of me.

I pulled myself up off the couch, groaning when my back muscles protested. "You right?" Scottie asked, concern lacing his voice.

"Fine," I groused. "Good night, everyone." I waved my hand as carelessly as I could manage and stumbled outside, waking up as soon as the cold night air hit my lungs. "Shit," I breathed, pulling my hood over my head as I hopped on one foot, tugging my boots on. Hopefully there were no spiders that'd taken residence in them, because I'd failed to even shake them out.

By the time I made it to the guesthouse, I was shivering and ready to climb into a warm bed. It was a shame I wasn't doing it with the one person I wanted in there with me. I barely had the door closed, the fire back up to a dull roar, and most of my clothes off before I was falling back into bed. The sheets were chilled, but the pillow was like a cloud and the mattress one you could sink into.

It could have been minutes or hours later when the bed shifted and cold air from the doona lifting made me shiver, until a strong arm wrapped around me and a cool body pressed against mine. "You're cold," I mumbled.

"I'm sorry," Scottie whispered between kisses along my neck and shoulder. I knew he meant more than just pulling me from my warm cocoon. His gentle caresses and the earnestness of his words let me know in no uncertain terms that he meant what he said too. He scooted closer so that there wasn't a hair's breadth between us, and I sighed, enjoying him being close.

I twined my fingers with his and replied, "I know I said we'd keep things between us secret. I get why you can't tell anyone about us, and that's fine. I'm not asking you to change that. But can you not act like one of those dickheads who picked on me in high school?" I yawned, my body telling me that my place right then was to be asleep in Scottie's arms. "I'm sorry I fell asleep in the first place."

"You don't have anything to be sorry for. Ally came back inside with Craig and Sam, and when she saw us, she smiled, and I panicked. I had every bad scenario running through my head and it freaked me out—"

"Like what?" I rolled over to face him, pressing my leg between his and holding him close. "Can I do anything to help?"

He shook his head, a sad smile on his face in the moonlight. "You can call me out on my bullshit. This thing between us can be complicated and messy. I can get scared and hide forever, or I can come out and live. It's going to take me a bit to get over this thing I have inside scaring the livin' daylights out of me, but I promise you that I'll come out, and I'll never treat you like that again."

"Okay." I nodded, touching his face with my fingertips. "I believe you. But I don't want you to come out for me. Do it for you. Do it because you're ready, not because you think I'll leave, because I won't. I love what we have exactly the way it is. Do I want to be able to reach out for you or cuddle on the couch? Absolutely. But you're worth waiting for, even if it means only getting to touch you at night like this. And I'll do it for as long as I need to."

Scottie shook his head, wonder brightening his eyes. "You're like the entire Milky Way in the night sky—you light up even the darkest places. I always want to be around your light." I brushed my lips against his and held him close. This right here, lying with him and talking, was perfection. I never wanted it to change. But I had to give him some space too. I knew our relationship wouldn't survive otherwise.

"We've spent a lot of time together over the last few weeks. Do you think we need to have some alone time during the day so we can be together at night without any-one thinking I follow you around like a puppy?"

"I don't give a fuck what Craig thinks."

"No, but if he's picked up on it, the others might have too. Do you want rumours starting around your own sta-tion? Maybe it'd be easier if we're a little more strategic about what time we spent together." I didn't know if that's what we needed, but it made sense that if we were to-gether constantly, we could get sick of each other. What was the saying? Absence makes the heart grow fonder?

"Like pacing ourselves?" Scottie hummed thoughtfully and brushed away a piece of hair that'd fallen in front of my eyes. "It's probably not a bad idea. But we'll need to spend a fair chunk of time together in a few weeks. I want you to come to Brissie with me."

"What for?" I asked, not giving him a chance to answer before pulling him in for a kiss. As our lips brushed together, I slipped my hand under his tee and ran my fingers down his spine, along the divot there. I loved touching him, loved be-ing in his arms. As long as I could do it, I'd be a happy man.

He pulled back slowly and nudged our noses together. "The Ekka. I'm taking down a few of our bulls and entering them into the agricultural competition. We do it every year, and I normally go alone, but this time I want you to come."

"I'd love to." I had visions of a hotel with white sheets—much like the ones we were currently buried under—room service, a pool, and a massage for Scottie's punished mus-cles. I doubted we'd have time for any of it, because we'd most likely be camping in the showgrounds so we were near the cattle, but we'd managed a few romantic camping trips so far.

"Good. I've booked us a hotel on the river." I grinned, and Scottie smiled. "You're easy to please, you know?"

"Is there a pool? A pool would make it perfect."

"There's one right on the river. Hopefully if we go late enough at night, we'll be the only people there." His grin turned lascivious and my cock perked up at the sight, my hole clenching too. But as sexy as it sounded, the reality sucked. Water was not a good lubricant.

"Have you ever had sex in a pool?" I scrunched up my nose. "It's not comfortable."

"No, but I wasn't thinking that. I was planning on seeing how long I could hold my breath for."

I groaned, my cock at half-mast and quickly thickening. Scottie pushed me onto my back and climbed on top in one swift motion, grinding down on me as he plundered my mouth. I spread my legs and held him tight, my hands moving to his arse to encourage him to keep moving. I took in a shaky breath when Scottie moved to my throat, biting and sucking on the sensitive skin there. He'd leave a mark low on my neck, and that turned me on more than I wanted to admit. With every brush of his fingertips, every pump of his hips, and every caress of his lips, I edged closer, but I never wanted it to end.

✦✦✦✦✦

"Righteo, we've got a busy day ahead of us," Scottie announced to the group as we sat around the table eating breakfast. A week had travelled fast, and Waru and Yindi were back with us. "Waru and Pete, can you please look at the horses today. Banjo cut his leg yesterday and I need it tended to again. You might as well check whether any of the horses need re-shoeing at the same time. Craig, Sam, and Ally, you're on feed duty. Jono and I are going to pick out the bulls we're taking to the Ekka so if you could check on the cows, that'd be great. Den and Yindi, can you please go over to Harrison's and pick up his float? I offered to service it for him if we could use it. He's not competing this year."

There were echoes of "Sure, boss," and "No worries" around the table. I just nodded and marvelled the way in which his family followed him. He was the boss, yes, but that wasn't why they did what he asked. They respected him, and they'd be loyal to him because of it.

My day with Waru was instructive. He was a funny bugger but so knowledgeable too. He didn't just get me to help him. He taught me the ropes. He showed me how to clean Banjo's hooves, the signs to look for when checking if he needed re-shoeing and how to care for his injury. The cut on Banjo's leg was still weeping, but it wasn't infected, so we cleaned and tended it before leaving him in the stable. We checked the fences and discovered a few wires that had sprung and were jutting out just enough to be dangerous for the horses. Finding it turned into an exercise of mending the fence, retying the wires that had come loose. It wasn't until we heard the bell ringing for lunch that we stopped, realizing the time. After lunch, I checked over the rest of the horses under Waru's supervision, and Waru showed me how to re-shoe two of them—Jono's horse, a mottled grey gelding called Stormy, and Waru's own, a mahogany-coloured mare, named Jedda, or "pretty girl" in English.

Sweaty from a day's work, I was on a high knowing I'd contributed in some small way to the running of the station. When I walked into the guesthouse just before dinner, I grinned at myself in the mirror before stripping down and bathing at the sink. The air was cooling fast, and I chose a fresh shirt and threw my woollen jumper over the top. I was on time for dinner for once, and I was starved.

Opening the door to the guesthouse, I heard grunting. Low and deep, but soft at the same time. I hadn't heard anything like it before. *What is it?* Whatever animal was there, it wasn't a snake.

That relief soon turned to laughter when the cutest wombat ever charged me as I stepped off the bottom step onto the red dirt. It was about the size of a medicine ball—bigger than a soccer ball by quite a bit—and I'd clearly pissed it off. Head down and bracing his legs like a crazy cartoon animal ready to launch out of the gates, it was fierce but adorable. When he took off, moving faster towards me than I'd ever imagined they could move, I shuffled back in shocked surprise. I didn't want to agitate it anymore, so I got out of his way. It disappeared under the house, and I heard more grunting and snuffling. I wondered if there was a burrow under there. If there was, we'd need to check it out. I wasn't sure how deep they went, but burrowing under the wrong part could cause the foundation to collapse, and we'd have a squashed wombat on our hands, and possibly some babies. I vaulted over the balustrade on the opposite side of the house and headed to the homestead, following my nose to dinner, the wombat on my mind.

Noise surrounded me with everyone milling in the dining room as I pushed through the door and closed it after me. I could smell the food outside, but from inside, it was delicious. Unmistakably casserole and fresh baked bread. Most of the hands were already filling their plates with it and the mashed potato and green veggies Ma and Nan had laid out. I groaned, my stomach rumbling hard as I breathed deep. "God, that has to be the best smell," I praised Ma as she handed me a plate. "Thanks for tea."

"My pleasure, love." She patted me on the back and passed another plate to Den, who'd walked in after me.

"Good day?" Den asked me as we moved over to the table.

"Yeah, mate. How was your trip?"

"Good. Tiring but. Sitting down for so long kills me," he replied, stretching out his back.

"How long a trip is it to wherever you went?"

"Next door neighbour's house? About a six-hour round trip."

I gaped at him. I wasn't sure I'd ever get used to the remoteness of this place, but that was what I loved most about it. Three hours to get to the next-door neighbour's.

"Oh, wow," I breathed. "Where are they? Like, which direction?"

"South-east. Instead of turning left to go to Longreach at the end of the drive, you turn right and head further down the road for an hour or so to get to the boundary of Pearce Station. They're the next ones along. Easy drive with it being so dry, but it's just long. Give me a day working instead of driving any day."

I shook my head and heaped my plate with food. Everyone had settled into their seats and were waiting for Den and me to sit down. "Sorry," I said to them, quickly taking my seat next to Scottie.

"Hey," he greeted me with a small smile. "How'd you fare today?"

"Learnt so much. Waru's a great teacher." I grinned at him and picked up a green bean, popping it into my mouth as Scottie nodded with a smile.

"Good to hear."

Conversation continued around me as we all ate, but I was quiet, happy to watch Scottie out of the corner of my eye. He got an update from everyone on their progress, made a concerned noise when Ally mentioned two of the cows were showing distress and the state of the grey kangaroos that had been resting in the shade near them. They were starving, dying of thirst too.

"I've been thinking about this for a while actually. I want to build an overflow trough low enough to the ground that the native animals can access it. We can't dig it in, or the animals could get stuck in it and drown, and I don't want to dig out dams or the evaporation will just make them boggy messes, and they'll be more danger than help. There's no natural watercourse here anymore, and the grass is pretty much dead. They're not getting the nutrients or the water they need. We can't stand by and do nothing."

Sam and Den looked at each other, Sam saying, "It's not a bad thing that there aren't as many roos around though," just as Den said, "We're gonna attract a few dingoes too, boss."

"They deserve to be looked after too, don't you think?" Scottie challenged them. "What about we look at one of the bores in the smaller paddock? The one we're retiring."

"I'll help build it," I volunteered.

Scottie smiled at me, and Ma added, "I think we should aim to do at least a few of the bores. Start with one that isn't being used, and once we perfect it, we can move onto the others. If the mines can use the Basin water in their operations, we can use it to sustain the native animals. We'll just have to design something that won't continuously empty the cattle trough into the pond, so it overflows."

"Auto shut-off valve would do it," Sam added.

Den spoke then, "We turn off the bores in the paddocks when we move the cattle out. We'd have to keep them on. We don't want both tanks being filled though. We might need to rig up a system where the lower tank will fill from the cattle tank and flow from one to the other is limited. Could be a complicated set-up, but doable."

"So if we water the animals, is there a way to feed them too?" I hedged. "I mean, I don't know whether we can or not, but is it worth looking at?"

"They become dependent on the feed then. If they gather in the same spot every day, it'll create a trap for them. Predators will lie in wait and it'll backfire on us."

They nutted it out over dinner, and as the plates were cleared away, we had a plan to contact the co-op in town, special order shallow tanks, and all the piping we'd need, together with the flow restrictors and auto shut-off valves. It was complex but ingeniously simple at the same time, and I was excited to start putting a test design into action when the materials were delivered.

EIGHT

Scottie

Sitting around the dinner table, hashing out how to make native animal watering holes a reality was brilliant. Energizing. I'd seen their decline myself and had been mulling over how to address it. The roos jumping past me and Pete while he was searching for gold were far too skinny. Even the big reds that weathered drought conditions so much better than the smaller greys were suffering. The dingoes were venturing closer to the herds, hunting in desperation for water, and the emus were poking around too. I'd seen more carcasses in the shortened muster we'd undertaken than we'd typically see on a full-length one. The problem had been staring me in the face the whole time, as had the solution. I'd thought about it when Pete and I were out at the bore together. I was almost kicking myself for not getting started earlier. But affording it was going to be a challenge. We were doing okay, but I could easily drop a hundred grand in equipment in an exercise like this without any return. It could ruin us financially if I outlaid that much while we were in a drought that had no end in sight.

I slumped down in the chair in the office and leaned my head back, rolling my neck and trying to ease some of the tension. I had a lot on my mind, and the Ekka had crept up on me this year. I wasn't well prepared for it; at least I didn't feel like I was. Should I even go? Should I forget about the competitions we'd entered? Queensland's agricultural show wasn't the biggest in Australia, but it was where we'd made some important industry connections that had served us well. We'd been supplying a nationwide chain of independent grocers for years now, together with one of the largest butchers in the country. And it was contract renewal time. They might not be there, and it'd be a waste of time going, but if the rep was and we weren't, we'd miss an important opportunity to directly compare the quality of our cattle against others in the region. Ultimately, the contract negotiations weren't conditional upon us going, but it never hurt to win a category or two. I'd always made it a point to look up our reps and catch up with them on their home turf as well as welcoming them to the station for their inspections. The drought had made me reconsider going to the Ekka, but it was more important than ever that we secure the contracts for another term.

The beginning of my headache was niggling at my temples, but it was my neck that was the problem. Tension tightened the muscles there into knots, and I groaned, trying to stretch it out with no success. The only way I'd reduce some of that tension was to get some work done and figure out where to from here. Knowing what I was up for and cash-flowing it would at least give me something to plan towards.

The door closing behind me made me wince, even the soft click sending a shard of pain through my head. The ambient noise from the loungeroom muted, and I sighed, thankful that it was quieter. Strong hands on my shoulders and Pete's fingers kneading into the muscle there had me groaning. I tilted my head to give him more room as he breathed on my neck, kissing a trail to my ear.

"What can I do to help?" he murmured.

"Keep doing that," I responded, leaning into him as he blanketed my back with his front and continued working the muscles down my arms.

"You're stressed." A kiss. "You take on too much." Kiss. "Let me shoulder some of it too." Another kiss.

I nodded. I was stressed, but it was my responsibility. How could I even think about handing it off to him? He paused his movements momentarily, but when I didn't speak, he continued, and asked, "How did you go today?" Pressing his fingers alongside my spine, kneading and rubbing out the knots made me hiss with pain. "Jesus, you're tense," he muttered, reaching forward to unbutton the top two buttons of my flannie. He pulled it up over my head and off, leaving me in just a singlet. That went too, and I sat there at the desk, shirtless. Pete's pause and soft hum had me smiling, thinking about something entirely different to what I had to be doing. Then his hands landed on my shoulders again and those magic fingers worked the knots out with a practiced touch.

"Where'd you learn that?" I asked, suddenly jealous of whatever man he'd performed it on.

"I did a massage course during one of my holidays at uni. Figured if I worked as a masseur, it might pay more than a crappy job at a hotel or in retail. Turns out that most jobs for male masseurs with basic qualifications like I had involved giving happy endings, and that's so not me. So, aside from the other students who I did the course with, you're the first person to get one." His words soothed the green-eyed monster inside, and I smiled, tilting my head back and puckering my lips. He obliged and brought his mouth to mine, kissing me slowly. "But I don't mind happy endings with you." I chuckled at that and spun, pulling him into my lap. The chair protested, creaking under our combined weight. As it was, I was probably too big for the little typist chair, but I didn't really care. Pete pressed his lips against mine again, moving to straddle me. Our tongues tangled and his warmth wrapped around me while we made out like horny teenagers. The whole time he didn't stop rubbing my knotted muscles.

The knock on the door startled us, and we didn't have a chance to move before it pushed open and Ma walked through. She took one look at us, mussed-up hair, lips kiss swollen, and me half-dressed, and muttered, "Don't break my chair, and don't screw on the desk," before backing out again and shutting the door.

Pete and I looked at each other and laughed before the chair tipped and we started falling. I held Pete close and grabbed the side of the desk, Pete mirroring my actions as we tried to halt our fall. But it was too late. The timber desk shifted as the chair hit the floor and I landed with a thud with Pete on top of me. He laughed harder, and I rolled, pushing the chair out from underneath me. Nestled between Pete's legs, I leaned down and kissed his still-laughing lips before another knock sounded. "You'd better not have broken my chair," Ma groused. I knew she didn't care about the chair. It was her way of asking if we were okay.

"Chair's still in one piece, relax," I called out, laughing again. "We're fine too. Thanks for asking."

"Uh-ha. Was going to ask if you wanted a cuppa. Now you can make it yourself," Ma teased.

"Mmm, coffee?" Pete breathed from below me, running his hands down my sides. "Or you?" I growled and turned my attention to him, lowering my weight onto him fully and kissing him again. He melted into me, wrapping his jean-clad legs around my hips and kissing me until I was drunk.

When we pulled back for a breath, Pete smiled. "You know there's no competition, right? Coffee will always be my first love." I scowled at him playfully, gripped his wrists, and lifted his hands above his head, then leaned down, keeping my mouth just out of reach of his. With my free hand, I tickled him until he was squirming and howling underneath me. "Oh my God, stop," he begged, between laughing and half-heartedly trying to break free. "Mercy!"

I threaded my fingers into his, holding both hands with mine and blanketed him with my body, bringing my lips to his again. We kissed—this time slower and longer, a promise of what would come later that night. But for now, I needed to get this paperwork done. Pete sensed the shift in my mood and loosened his hold, cupping my face and running his socked foot down my calf.

"Tell me how I can help. Please."

"I'm just stressed. It's okay."

"No, it's not." He shook his head, his eyes full of concern. "Talk to me."

"Jono and I picked out a few bulls. We got them separated and mustered them in. They're in the holding yard now. They look good. Healthy. We've got a strong chance at placing, maybe even winning the categories we've entered. But we've got so much going on here that I'm not sure if our going is a good idea. On top of that, our supply contract with IGA is up soon. The rep might be there so I should be there too—you know, meet on his turf—and getting another contract would secure our income for a few more years. Those feeding ponds are gonna be expensive, so...."

"When would you normally leave for the Ekka?" he asked, running his fingers through my hair and scraping blunt nails along my scalp. I groaned in pleasure, the motions helping the headache that had faded into the background with our joking around.

"Two weeks. It's a fifteen-hour drive, so we have to do it over a couple of days. I can't drive that long in one go."

"What about with two of us driving? Would that help?"

I nodded. "It would, but have you ever driven with a float before?"

"I've never even driven with a trailer. But I could practice over the next week or so. If you're comfortable, then I could help you. If not, I make a great navigator."

"It's a straight road." I grinned. "But sure, okay."

"Right, so meeting with the rep and getting this contract renewed. Should we call your solicitor and ask them to follow up IGA for it? Or is that not how it's done?"

"We've always just waited for them to give it to us." I shrugged, which was difficult with me holding my weight over Pete while we laid on the floor.

"What about we go to them with a plan? Find out the costings of the tanks and other stuff you need and draw up a proposal for them." I furrowed my brow and was just about to interrupt Pete when he lifted his pointer finger up, silencing me. "Explain what you want to do and ask them if they want to renew so you can plan the expenses out. Don't ask them to fund it, but explain how, with their contribution through a renewed contract, they could be helping the wildlife. I don't know whether it'd be better coming from the solicitor or you in a phone call to the rep, but either way, securing a contract with them will take that stress off you, won't it?"

"Yeah, it would." I leaned down and pressed my lips to his. Just a soft, chaste kiss in thanks. When I pulled back, his smile, so full of love, took my breath away. He leaned up and kissed me again, and I moaned as he slipped his tongue into my mouth. I wanted to feel him skin on skin, so I slipped my hand under his woollen jumper.

"Uh-uh." He pulled back and sucked in a breath, and I froze. "I really want you to, but I have one more thing I want to ask before you undress me and all my brain cells dissolve into mush. Have you looked at drought assistance?"

I couldn't help my huff of laughter at his comment, but I became serious quickly. From what Den had told me, my neighbour Frank Harrison was doing it tough. In the hour that Den and Yindi had been there, they'd noticed a few things—the bare cupboards, the empty fridge. They didn't want to even drink the tea that Mary had set out in case it was their last pot. The old man was struggling to put food on the table for his wife and one remaining hand. Their land was even more devoid of fodder than ours, and their cattle had dwindled to a level that couldn't sustain them from the income they'd make. Their barn was empty of feed too, and the cows hanging around close to the house were starving. "No, there are plenty of people worse off than us. We've still got some savings. The other graziers need it way more than we do."

"This isn't a competition on how bad people have it. It's not charity. The government is offering help because cattle stations like yours feed our country. Our whole population needs your stations healthy. You should apply for it. The other station owners can look after their lot."

"I'm worried about Harrison," I blurted, not really acknowledging my need to do something to help until that moment. "He's been a grazier for decades and Den said he wasn't in good shape. I don't know that he can look after his lot." I shook my head. "I feel like I need to do something to help him, but I don't know what."

Pete was quiet a moment. "What about starting with a phone call? Ask if he's okay. Maybe he could do with a friend."

"You're a good man, Pete. You know that?" I nudged my nose against his and gasped when he bucked his hips, his hardening cock sliding against my own. "I think the paperwork can wait."

"Sounds like a bloody good idea," he rasped.

"Frank, g'day, mate," I said into the handpiece of the old home phone after breakfast the next morning. The line to my closest neighbour was crackly but still clear enough to hear. We didn't speak often, and I lamented that a bit. Frank and Pops had had a falling out years earlier, but he'd been there to help Nan and Ma when Pops died. He and Mary were in between Ma and Nan's age, except unlike our family whose generations had stayed on the land, all of Frank and Mary's six kids had left. Their station was unsaleable in this drought, except to some foreign company with money to park offshore looking to snap up more agricultural land, and I doubted they'd sell it anyway. There was likely no way out for them. Their kids and grandkids were all city folk now, and from what I'd heard down the grapevine, they didn't venture out this way very often at all. Maybe if they did, they'd understand how tough their parents were doing it.

"Scottie, how are you?" he answered warmly. He'd aged since I'd last spoken to him, the warble in his voice more pronounced.

"Well, thanks. I wanted to call and say thanks for lending me the float." I hesitated, then continued in a rush, "And to check in, ask how you were doing. We don't speak as often as we should, so I wanted to fix that."

"Oh, yeah, no worries. Keep it for as long as you need it. There's no rush getting it back to us."

"Probably three weeks if that's okay," I responded. "How's Mary?"

"She's okay for an old bird." He chuckled, and I heard a shuffling before Mary came on the line.

"I'll give you old bird," she muttered before Frank laughed, and the screen door slamming shut sounded in the background. She grumbled something under her breath and then spoke to me. "How are you, Scottie? I was just telling Frank that we should call you more often than we do. We wanted to thank you for sending Dennis and Yindi over, too. We've been having trouble with the tractor, and Yindi took a look under it and fixed the problem within a few minutes. None of us could get under there."

"I'm glad they could help. You know if you ever need anything like that, we're only a phone call away? I don't mind sending over whoever you need to help out, especially with only the three of you tending to your mob."

"Thanks, Scottie we appreciate that." I heard a sniffle through the line and hoped that she wasn't crying. How long had it been since someone offered them assistance?

"How are things otherwise, Mary? You three doing okay?" I asked.

"We're getting by. The cattle are doing it tough. There's just not enough feed left. We've lost a few, and I don't know how much longer we'll be able to keep ordering bales. We should be selling the entire mob, but don't tell Frank I said that. He's a stubborn old bastard. Thinks he can keep running this place on hope alone."

"Mary, how can I help?" Even I could hear the pleading in my voice, but I wasn't ashamed of it. I just hoped they wouldn't be too embarrassed or proud to accept it.

"I don't know that anyone can, darl." This time her sniff was more pronounced. For this woman to be crying on the phone to me—a neighbour, but a relative stranger too—they were in dire straits. I'd never seen the strength of any of the station owners out here waver, but the weather was bad. "We've lost nearly everything."

"I've never experienced anything like this drought before."

"It's something, isn't it," she lamented.

"Have you looked at the assistance package the government's offering? I think it could help with feed and transport."

"No, Frank didn't want to take charity, but we're on our last legs here, Scottie. I can't bear to see the cattle dying."

"You know, a friend said to me that it isn't a competition on how bad things are out here, and it's not charity because we feed the country. People like us need to be healthy to make sure that Australia is healthy. I think he's right." I winced, thinking of Pete as a friend. God, I wanted to come out and be proud of what I was—who I was—but I couldn't.

Not yet. Maybe not ever. I closed my eyes, grateful that my sexuality was my biggest problem, and guilty that I wasn't even brave enough to face it when people and animals were literally starving out here in the desert.

"He sounds like he knows what he's talking about."

"He does. He's a good man too, so he's not pulling my leg. Do you want my help applying for it?"

"I... I might need help with the forms." She paused, and her voice was quiet when she spoke again, filled with shame. "We don't have internet anymore. They disconnected it and I can't see well these days either. Think I need some glasses."

"I'll be out there later today. I'll get the forms and we'll go through them together, okay? I can submit them online for you too."

"Bless you, Scottie," she cried, soft sobs through the line. I closed my eyes, powerlessness overcoming me. Blinking away my own tears, I blew out a breath and went out into the loungeroom. Ma was vacuuming but turned the old machine off as soon as she saw me on the phone.

"I'm always happy to help. I'll stock up on some emergency supplies for you and bring them with me, okay. Expect us in about five hours."

"I don't know how to thank you."

"Don't," I said gently. "It's not necessary. That's what we do for each other." We said our goodbyes and I hung up, slumping down onto the couch with my head hung low.

"Who was that?" Ma asked, coming to sit next to me.

"Mary. They're in trouble, Ma. Frank's too proud or stubborn to ask for help, and meanwhile, their cattle are starving and so are they. Den told me yesterday that everything's in poor shape. I rang this mornin' to say thanks and see how they were doing and they're on their last legs."

We worked out a plan. Ma called in Nan to cook up a storm and I went for Jono. If anyone knew cattle, it was him. I needed him with me to go over their herd and make sure we didn't need the vet out there. Waru was better with horses so I had him get some tools and come with us. By the time we were ready to head out, Ma and Nan had a couple of meals made, and they'd filled an esky with fruit, vegetables, and meat and another bag with canned foods. Pete and Sam had dropped as many bails as would fit into the trailer, and Yindi had included her toolbox in the boot of the Landcruiser. It looked like the four of us were going, and we'd probably be camping out under the moonlight. Mary and Frank's station was much smaller than ours, and they'd never had staff quarters like we did. Their one or two stockmen had always slept in cots on the enclosed veranda or in the bedrooms once the kids had moved out. But that was okay. We'd slept many a night under the stars.

The four-by-four was packed up and the trailer, piled high with feed, was connected. All that remained was for us to head off. Pete wandered over and our gazes snagged. "You guys nearly set?" he asked.

"Yeah, but I'm heading to the dunny before we go." I motioned to the house and strode off.

"Yeah, um, I need to…," Pete muttered, not finishing his sentence. I heard his quick footsteps on the hard-packed earth behind me. We weren't subtle about it, but I needed a private moment with him, especially since waking up next to him that morning and watching the sunrise together. I was being reckless, I knew that. Fear still strangled me every time I thought about anyone knowing about us. But at the same time, I almost wanted to be found out. If we were, it'd be a relief. Ironic given all the trouble it'd likely cause.

I headed straight for my bedroom, Pete following me. As soon as he entered, I closed the door and pulled him into my arms, breathing him in and holding him as close as I could. "I'm so proud of you," he whispered against the skin of my throat.

I furrowed my brow, confusion washing over me, and I pulled away until I could look at him. "For what?"

"Are you serious?" He smiled, adoration in his eyes. I couldn't help but smile at him in return. He lit me up inside like the sun's warm rays. "I told you to call them to see if they needed a friend, and in a few hours, you've marshalled together food, supplies, and labour like you're mounting a rescue mission."

"They did it for us when Pop died. And even if they didn't, they're good people. They don't deserve to suffer."

"You were stressed out last night with everything on your plate and you've put all that to one side. You're doing your neighbours a solid. I don't know a better man than you, Scottie." I didn't reply. I couldn't. My throat had constricted, and I just wanted to feel him in my arms. I breathed him in again and smelt fresh hay, sweat, and something that was uniquely Pete. I groaned and kissed a line up his throat, tasting the saltiness on his skin.

"We'll be away overnight, at least," I murmured.

"It'll be good for us too," he added, carding his fingers through my hair. "But I'll still miss you."

"Same." He kissed me then, long and slow until we were out of breath. I pulled back, sure the others would come looking if I didn't get a move on.

"Be careful, okay." Pete cupped my face in his hands and brushed his lips softly against mine, a chaste kiss to say goodbye. When I nodded, he did it again and smiled softly, before walking out so that we exited separately. By the time I joined the others, Jono was in the driver seat, Yindi next to him, and Waru behind her. The only spot left was behind Jono, the seat with the least legroom. It served me right for taking so long, and I shot a smirk to Pete as he closed the door after me. "Drive safe," he called out as he tapped the door frame and stepped away from the Landcruiser.

"He's a good bloke that one," Jono said absently as we pulled away, and I couldn't help but agree. I hoped they still had the same opinion of him—and me—if they ever found out about us. I inhaled, breathing in the dusty air swirling around us and let the thoughts tumble around in my head. But all the what-ifs and buts fell away when I thought about Pete. The road before us would be rough, not a single part of it a smooth ride, but the more I thought on it, the more I wanted Pete sitting next to me as I made the journey. Until he'd come along, I was existing, not living, and I wouldn't really be able to start living until I could live honestly with those I considered family.

Hours passed and the landscape seemed to die before my eyes. Where my station was covered with dead grass and big eucalypts, the landscape at the boundary of Harrison Station was barren. It was as if the desert was swallowing all the life around it. Cracks in the hard-packed earth were visible even from the road, and the old eucalypts in the distance were long dead, their faded grey trunks devoid of any vegetation. Sadness overwhelmed me. I loved the red dirt and blue skies. The landscape was part of me, my blood bled that red dirt. It was entwined with my existence in a way most people didn't understand. But this... this was heartbreaking. This dirt was lifeless.

We pulled up at the homestead. The dirty-white building, its paint peeling and rusting roof stood stark against the vibrant landscape. The trio standing on the front steps of the old Queenslander were showing their age. Dressed similarly, their clothes were all old and tattered, but that wasn't what stood out to me. It was the weight on their shoulders, like a physical load they were carrying, causing them to haunch over. "Let's do what we can here to help," I said quietly so only my companions in the Landcruiser could hear despite the open windows. "Anything major that needs to be done, make a note of it and speak to me about it privately. I'll see what resources we can spare and reapply them here."

Stepping out of the Landcruiser, I took a closer look at Frank, Mary, and their hand, Bill. Tired lines creased both

Frank and Bill's foreheads, and Mary's cheeks were hollowed out. I hoped it wasn't because of a lack of food, but I knew better. I also knew people like these three wouldn't appreciate being called out on it. "G'day, mate," I greeted Frank, holding my hand out to him as I approached the steps. "Hope you don't mind, I brought some bits and pieces with me, and the others wanted to come out and see whether they could be of use to you."

"We don't want your charity, Scottie," Frank chastised me. He reached for my hand and added, "But I'm mighty appreciative of you ignoring my stubbornness and offering to help anyway."

"Anything I can do." And that's what we did for the next two-and-a-bit days. I repaired fences and mended things in the barn, moving around some of the heavier equipment and broken pieces to get them out of the way. Yindi looked at the vehicles and worked on the nearby bores, fixing problems with the mechanisms high up on the windmill while Jono and Waru cared for the cattle and horses. In the evening, we went through the paperwork, and I helped them apply for the drought assistance and on the hush-hush, I called in a favour with the doc to have him and his nurse visit. The more time I'd spent with Mary, the more I was convinced she wasn't doing so well.

Leaving their station, I felt like I'd contributed something small to help them. It would be a long road ahead for all of us, but I wouldn't make the mistake of forgetting my neighbours again. Especially not when they had no one else.

We were met by Pete and Ma sitting on rocking chairs, blankets wrapped around their shoulders and across their laps when we pulled up to our homestead late in the evening. My man grinned as I closed the car door and he crossed over to us, a blanket in each hand as we approached. It'd been a cold few days, the temperatures dropping to frigid before the cooler temperatures were finally laid to rest. As spring progressed, it would bring with it the blazing sun. Hopefully the wet season would make an appearance too. We were dependent on monsoon rains from up north travelling through the network of dried riverbeds to reach us. The long-term forecast didn't show much by way of direct rain, but if we didn't have hope, what did we have?

Pete passed me a blanket and gave the other to Waru, who'd been sitting behind me. He rubbed his hands together, shivering slightly. "You're cold. Take it." I wrapped my blanket around Pete's shoulders and let my hand brush along his, catching his fingertips momentarily before letting go. The smile he gave me was radiant, and I would have done almost anything to be able to wrap him in my arms and kiss him properly.

"Hi," he murmured, still smiling. In the dim light from the homestead veranda, I could see his blush.

Placing my hand low on his back, I walked him the long way around the vehicle and now empty trailer, wishing no one would notice if we just kept going straight into the guesthouse. "Hi," I whispered back, leaning closer to him and squeezing his hip. A full-body shudder ripped through him, and I added, "Your bed tonight. We'll need the privacy."

NINE

Pete

Scottie drove away from the homestead slower than he would ordinarily take the dirt driveway, but the bulls in his charge were precious. Potentially prize-winning. It was more than that though. He genuinely cared about their welfare, not just their money-making capacity.

It was early; the sun still an hour away from rising. The headlights of the Landcruiser cut into the darkness around us, demarking the safe path along the red dirt drive. But beyond that, the blackness enveloped us. We were on our way to Brisbane for the Ekka, the Royal Queensland Show, and I was excited. Not so much to be back in a city, but because we were going to present a plan to the IGA rep who Scottie had a meeting with. We'd all contributed to it. Sam and I had worked together to draw up blueprints, turning Scottie's model test pond that he'd almost singlehandedly built into a concrete plan. Each of the ponds had an auto-feeder and an auto-stop valve to prevent wastage. Ally had done all the research. Every potential government grant, environmental regulation around the use of the Basin's water, and restrictions on feeding native animals had been covered off. Ma and Nan had priced out all the materials and applied for every one of the grants Ally identified. Jono, Den, and Craig had fed the animals and mucked out sheds. Their routine included checking over the cows daily as they wiled away their days in the more confined paddocks, the springer paddock—which still measured bigger than some suburbs—that they would spend their time while in calf. Once we were all satisfied, I'd transferred everything onto a CAD program and pulled the report together, creating a business plan that we would present to the IGA rep. Scottie was adamant that the plan made it clear that he wasn't asking for funding, but rather announcing his proposals and inviting them to be a part of it through a contract renewal.

But for the moment, I was enjoying the beginning of the drive, sitting next to my man and watching him as he concentrated on driving. We'd swap over in a few hours, giving Scottie a chance to catch a nap if he needed it. In the couple of weeks since he'd announced we were going to the Ekka, I'd hitched up the float and driven more kilometres getting used to it than I'd spent behind the wheel in the six months prior on Sydney roads. I still wasn't an expert in parking the thing but driving forwards I could do.

The quiet of the pre-dawn was soothing, but soon enough, the sun was up and we were reaching the halfway point of the trip. We'd driven through some of the most famous outback towns in Queensland. Quilpie was known for its opals, and it was where I'd dropped off my metal detector. I hoped whatever was wrong with it was easy enough to fix. We'd also passed through Charleville, home of the western Queensland operations of Cobb & Co, the stagecoach manufacturers. We were stopping at Mungallala, a tiny outpost that was home to less than 150 people and about halfway to Brisbane. The caravan park was more of a fenced-in paddock with a couple of nice-looking caravans parked near an amenities block with two toilets and a shower. Scottie led us in the opposite direction, moving to the farthest corner of the park and bringing the float around to the temporary fencing that had been erected.

"The bulls will stay in there tonight." He pointed to the area behind the fence with pockets of dry grass. "The owners set it out for us, so we didn't have to do the full trip in a day."

We stayed overnight there, sleeping in our swags, much to the dismay of the owners. They'd offered us one of the caravans, but Scottie refused, telling them we'd need to keep watch over the bulls to make sure they didn't try to get past the fences through the night. I knew the real reason—we'd give new meaning to the old saying "if the van's a rockin'."

Within a couple of hours of leaving the next day, we'd passed through Roma and another seven hours later we were at the bustling RNA showgrounds in Brisbane. I hadn't taken the same route to get to Pearce Station, instead travelling up the coast and then west to Longreach before driving south-west to the station. The whole trip was all new terrain for me, and I'd loved it. Wide-eyed, I'd taken in every minute of the evolving landscape, watching it change from red dirt to sub-tropical city.

The sounds and smells of the Ekka surrounded us. Fresh hay and feed, animals and whip cracks, the testing of the rides as the roadies set them up. In twelve hours, the rides would be full, the gleeful—or terrified—squeals of the riders as they were spun and flipped in the air being heard far and wide. The faint scent of deep-fried food—dagwood dogs, doughnuts, and chips—and sugar would permeate the air. Fairy floss was a favourite. I wasn't sure whether we'd have a chance to walk around, or whether we'd be staying with the animals the whole time, but I didn't much mind.

The only thing I wanted at that point was a shower at the hotel we were staying in. But that didn't happen for hours. By the time we had the bulls out of the float and settled into the sheds, watered and fed as well as having filled out all the paperwork and had an inspection from the onsite supervisors, we were both exhausted, sweaty, and otherwise filthy. Scottie blew out a breath and dug out the keys from his pocket to the big Landcruiser. We'd unhooked the float and stored it and were about to head into Teneriffe, a five-minute drive away on the river. I looked at him and smiled. "Want me to drive? I'm used to cities."

"Oh, thank God," he breathed, handing me the keys. "Knock yourself out." He programmed the nav for me and we headed off on the short trip. The hotel we were staying in was full of old-world charm. It was a renovated wool store filled with original brickwork, thick timber beams, high ceilings, and loads of natural light from the factory-sized windows. Polished timber floors overlaid with plush rugs and flowing white curtains gave the mix of old industrial and modern, a soft feel with an undisputed elegance. I looked down at my ratty tee and filthy jeans and groaned. I didn't want to touch a thing in case I stained it, especially not the pristine white linen on the bed in the room we'd just checked into.

"You want to get room service, and shower while we wait for it?" Scottie asked me as we walked into the bathroom together. We came to a halt at the same time, both spying the massive bath. I had a feeling that the last time Scottie would have sunk into water up to his neck was his visit to Sydney earlier in the year—although, given New South Wales was drought-affected too, maybe not. I didn't even bother suggesting it. Instead, I pushed in the plug, emptied a single-use container of the bubble bath into it and began filling it so we could soak.

"Room service can wait, I think," I mused as Scottie stripped. Everything came off except his hat. He went naked to the minibar and snagged the miniature bottle of bubbles and a couple of glasses, bringing them over to the ledge. Within minutes, we were sinking into the heavenly hot water, Scottie luxuriating in my arms as water lapped up over his thighs.

"This water is orgasmic," he mumbled, using his foot to flick off the tap to halt the flow of water. His eyes were closed, his head resting on my shoulder. I ran the sudsy washcloth over his skin, following the path with my other hand. Warm muscle rippled under my palm, and he groaned in pleasure with my gentle strokes. His semi poked above the waterline, but I ignored it in favour of cleaning every part of my man that I could reach. I filled my palm with shampoo and massaged his head, Scottie making the most obscene noises as I scratched my blunt nails along his scalp and tugged on the strands of his hair. He shuddered, his cock getting harder before my eyes.

"You like this, huh?" I murmured. "You want my hands on you?" I teased, moving my hands down to tweak his nipples. Scottie shifted against me, and there was no mistaking my erection pressing against his back.

"Fuck," he muttered, arching his back. Water sloshed about us as I trailed my fingertips down his abs and brought them back up until he was fidgeting under my ministrations. He whimpered, and I couldn't help my chuckle. "Pete," he growled, gasping as I closed my fist around his length. Working him over, Scottie shifted against me, snaking his hand behind him and jacking my cock as best he could. I groaned, wanting more contact with him. Wanting to be buried inside him, or to have him deep in me. "This isn't bloody working," he muttered, huffing impatiently. Picking up the champagne glass off the counter, he downed the contents before dipping it in the water and tipping it over his head, repeating it until the suds were washed away. Spinning so he was kneeling between my spread legs, he soaped his hand up and washed me. His movements were fast but gentle. No nonsense. I chuckled and groaned when he pressed his thumbs into my hips and shuddered when he rubbed there, gasping when he continued the motion. He knew that of all the places on my body, it was the one spot that would get me going. Every time. Guaranteed.

"Jesus," I panted. "You're gonna make me come without even touching my dick."

"Get dry and get on the bed, Pete. We're not finished here." By the time I made it out of the bathroom, Scottie was already on the bed, and there was no doubt what he wanted. Legs spread and kneeling, his arse half hung off it. He had his chest pressed into the white bed linen, presenting himself to me like a damn buffet. There was no way I wasn't taking the opportunity to devour him whole. Like a fine wine, I sampled every part of him, starting at his nape and kissing the smooth skin along each vertebra, until I reached the curved globes of his arse. I nipped him on each cheek, licking away the sting, and then down his legs. Shifting along his crack, I let him feel the rasp of my stubble on his sensitive skin. I worked my way closer to his hole, tormenting us both with anticipation until finally, it was too much.

He choked out a moan and thrust his arse back at me, his pink pucker clenching as a full-body shudder passed through him. His body was begging me for more, even if his words were inarticulate, and the final thread of my control snapped. Grasping his cock from between his legs, a pearl of pre-cum dotting its slit, I licked him from tip to his balls, moaning as the salty pre-cum hit my tongue. Down over his seam and to that sensitive patch of hairless skin behind his balls. Around his hole, I lashed my tongue, slicking the way for my fingers to soften the muscle there. I held his cheeks apart and feasted on him, taking my fill as Scottie grunted incoherently before me. I loved seeing him reduced to guttural moans and cries of pleasure, unable to form any words. A sachet of lube and a condom was thrust at me, Scottie's unsubtle way of telling me to hurry the hell up while he was mindless with lust.

I didn't hesitate, suiting up and coating lube all over my length before pressing my tip against him, rimming his hole to lube him up. He arched his back, the curve in his spine enticing. I ran my hands along his sides, bringing them to his hips and psyching myself not to blow as soon as I entered him. Grasping myself in one hand, I guided my shaft into him, pressing forward slowly to let Scottie get used to the intrusion. It didn't take long before the perfect man before me blew out a breath and melted into the bed, going pliant under my hands. I slid forward, and he cried out when the angle allowed me to tag his prostate on my first pass. Heat surrounded me, snug and slick, and my eyes rolled back in my head as pleasure, intense enough to wipe out all my brain cells, blanketed me.

I was acting on instinct alone. Purely chasing the ecstasy of release for both of us. Wanting Scottie right there with me when I fell. No, needing him there. Touching every inch of his smooth skin, I plastered myself against his back, kissing him everywhere I could reach. All the while I rolled my hips in a slow grind. Every thrust, every breath against his skin, every nerve ending connecting, and exploding in sensation drove me higher. I was on the edge, but there was no way I was coming unless Scottie was right there with me. I reached around and grasped him. He shuddered in my hold after a couple of strokes, his release coating my hand and the bed below as he cried out. His arse muscles clenched as he did and it tossed me over, sending me into an oblivion I wasn't sure I wanted us to find our way back from. I fell forward, resting my forehead on his sweaty skin as we came down, catching our breaths together. His hole fluttered around me in an aftershock, and I groaned. When he chuckled, the vibration travelled through him into me. Replete, I ran my fingertips along his chest, spreading his sticky release over him before I cupped his balls and softened cock.

"Ungh," Scottie groaned into the mattress.

"Sorry, I'm probably squashing you."

He laughed again and shook his head. "No, but I can't feel my legs. Although that could have something to do with coming as hard as I did." I gripped the condom as I slid out of him and laid a kiss on his back before going to the attached bathroom to clean up and get a warm washcloth for Scottie.

My stomach rumbled just as I was climbing onto the bed behind him. "I'm starving too," Scottie sighed, having rolled to the side. "But I still can't move."

I put the order in, and within half an hour, we each had a steak and chips and a shared Caesar salad. We ate, sprawled out on the bed, naked once more with the TV showing the news in the background. We ignored it for the most part, but it gave us the ambient light we needed.

Scottie's meeting with the IGA rep was the next morning, so after dinner, he pulled out the plan and read over it a final time, even with his eyelids drooping. There was no need for him to worry. He knew its contents from cover to cover, every detail memorized. But it meant a lot to him and he was nervous. I quizzed him, asking the questions I thought the rep would ask until I proved to him that he could handle it.

"Will you come tomorrow?" he asked, his eyes closed and the plan on the floor beside the bed.

"Will it be weird with me there? I don't want to intrude on a business meeting."

Scottie cracked an eyelid open and shook his head, pursing his lips as if I was being ridiculous, but the words he said didn't match his expression. Instead, they were quiet and full of vulnerability. "I want you there. Please."

I kissed his shoulder, snuggled in closer, and nodded. "Then I'd love to be there."

The meeting was informal, held while standing by the pens housing the bulls. Scottie had introduced me to the rep, an older bloke, but one who was clearly experienced. He was struggling too, coughing into his elbow almost non-stop. Mark, the rep, knew his cattle, and he had a keen eye, commenting on the quality of the stocks represented at the Ekka with practiced ease. When Scottie had handed over a bound copy of the report, he'd read the summary and looked over the diagrams, questioning Scottie on the purpose and what the desired goals were. He'd raised an eyebrow when Scottie had explained that it didn't matter which animals the water attracted because all of them deserved water to sustain them.

"So you aren't worried about the wild dogs? What sort of culling do you have for the mixed-breeds?"

"None. We don't cull anything. They don't usually get near the homestead and so far this breeding season, we haven't had any troubles with them. During calving, we patrol the paddocks. The headlights and engine noise on the four-wheelers are usually enough to keep them away. This season might not be enough though, so we'll have to see how we go."

"And the roos? What about the damage they cause?"

Scottie laughed. "This is their land. I can't in good conscience say that they're causing damage to our agricultural land when they're native to the region. The roos are there because it's their habitat. Their eating the grass and feed is to be expected."

"Huh." He nodded. "You'd spoken about sustainability when I was out at the station last, but I suppose I didn't realize you meant anything except saving water. This is so much more thorough. This is environmental protection at a grassroots level. Accessibility to habitat for native animals, resting larger tracts of land from over-trampling by the cattle, alternative means to protect cattle from predators." He seemed impressed. "And do you still allow the local tribes access?"

"Absolutely." Scottie nodded.

"I want to take this plan back to the big bosses. We're drawing up your contract renewal now, but I think this needs to be factored in. IGA, as an organization, has made a commitment to supporting our suppliers to improve their sustainability, and you've blown me away with your approach on this." He shook his head and huffed out a breath. "I'm so impressed, Scott."

The smile that spread over Scottie's face stole my breath, and it took everything in me to resist wrapping my arms around him and whooping in delight. "Thanks, mate." Scottie held out his hand, and Mark shook it.

"As soon as I'm out your way, I'll come and check out that test tank you've built." They said their goodbyes, and I didn't hesitate, pulling Scottie to me and giving him the biggest bro-hug I could muster, complete with back-slapping.

"That's awesome, Scottie. Well done."

The icing on the cake would have been a win. Scottie didn't get that one, but he was close. The winning bulls were from a station up north. They'd been in drought up until the beginning of the year when the whole of northern Queensland was hit by a monsoon low that hung around and caused havoc. The flooding was so widespread that a few stations lost their entire herds; there was no ground high enough for some of them. The surviving bulls from that station had won, and Scottie was the first person in line to shake the bloke's hand. Mingling with the other station reps afterward was a good chance for Scottie to catch up with old mates, some from his days as a student of the School of the Air, and others he only knew from his visits to the Ekka. He'd kept me close, introducing me to his friends as a guest of the station who'd loved it and never left. I was an outsider there, but all of the people we spoke to were open and warm. All lamented the drought, all were frustrated by the lack of action in Canberra, but no one had any real solutions. They were continuing to do things the way they'd always been done. They produced high-quality cattle, but at a significant environmental impact.

By the time we'd wrapped up that afternoon, I was glad to get out of there. My quota of networking with people, when half of them were sick, had dried up hours earlier, and Scottie looked exhausted too. I'd dragged him away when he'd pressed his fingers against his temples for the third time, groaning when the laughter around us boomed out.

We weren't staying for the entire length of the show. Most of the cattle being judged in the early competitions would rotate out, making room for the next set of competition entrants. It meant we had one more night in our hotel room before beginning the journey home the next day. Home. When had I started referring to it as that? Possibly from the first moment I'd stepped foot onto Pearce Station. Possibly even earlier than that. As soon as I'd zoomed in, looking on the sprawling desert, I'd been drawn to the rich red dirt. I had no idea that the man standing next to me would be the reason to keep me there, but as far as striking it rich went, I'd hit the jackpot with him.

Scottie fumbled the swipe card for the room as I trailed my lips up his throat and nibbled on his earlobe. Wrapping my arms around him, I held him close, loving the way he tilted his head and hooked his hand around the back of my head, keeping me close so I could lick and suck on his skin.

The privacy of the empty hallway made us both a lot braver than we'd dared be in the showgrounds. We stumbled through the doorway when Scottie finally got it open, and he spun, walking backwards into the room. He pulled me closer, bringing my mouth down to his, and he devoured me. Scottie pushed me up against the door, his hands on my face and his mouth never leaving mine. I was taller, but his size and his presence overwhelmed me in the best possible way.

I was dreaming that I was a vulcanologist. Or maybe Frodo, tossing the ring into molten magma. Lava bubbled around me, searing my skin. But why was there an octopus with me? I woke, confused. But neither the octopus, nor the volcano, disappeared as I gained consciousness. It was as if I was in a furnace. One that was shivering and wrapped around me, clinging to me as if I was the only source of warmth around. Sweat poured off me, so when I reached out, I couldn't tell whether it was Scottie that was clammy or me. But he was hot, even warmer than he usually was when he slept. I pressed my hand against his forehead and sucked in a breath. He wasn't hot. He was feverish. "Scottie." I shook him, trying to wake him. "You're burning up."

"No, I'm cold." A shudder passed over him, wracking his body. "Really cold."

"It's not—" I didn't finish the sentence. Instead, I prised myself away from his arms and slid out from between his legs, narrowly dodging him when he reached out, trying to pull me back. Stumbling from the bed, I nearly landed on my arse as I tripped over the clothes that were still strewn across the floor after his knees were bruised, and I'd banged my head one too many times on the door as he deepthroated me. Our party for two had continued on the bed, resulting in twisted sheets and bitten pillows in an effort to save the neighbours from our marathon. We'd passed out, using tissues on the bedside table to wipe ourselves down and what might have been a spare pillow too. We'd leave a tip for the housekeeping staff, even though it wasn't customary in Aus.

But now, as I ran the washcloth under the tap, I tried to think about why he was sick. There was only one explanation—he'd caught a bug at the Ekka. Everyone around us had been sick. The place was like a lucky dip for germs. Shaking hands and touching railings had passed on those buggers quicker than I'd thought. I squeezed out the excess water and tentatively stepped around the clothes littering the floor so I could press it to his forehead. Scottie's sigh sounded like more of a groan.

Ma had insisted we take some paracetamol and ibuprofen with us, telling me that if the cattle were in pens near the loudspeakers, we'd appreciate it. And I had. The announcers' voices boomed while the hum of the crowd, punctuated by babies crying and children screaming, had a low-level headache buzzing around my head within hours of the first day. Scottie hadn't fared any better either. I just hoped we had a few left. I rummaged around, digging into the bottom of the backpack I'd taken with me the day before. My fingers closed around the pill packet and it crackled as I yanked it out.

I turned the light on in the bathroom, leaving the door ajar as I left with a glass of water and two paracetamol for him. It was just after two in the morning. Our alarm would be going off in less than two hours, but we wouldn't be going anywhere unless I could get Scottie's fever down.

Next to him on the bed again, I lifted the facecloth and touched his forehead. He was still burning up, the wet cloth warmed through. "Scottie," I whispered as I shook him lightly. "I need you to take these pills. You've got a fever. We need to get it down."

He cracked open one eye, squinting at the light emanating from the bathroom before groaning. "My throat. Feels like I've swallowed nails."

"I'll get you some tea. It'll help." I handed him the two paracetamol and waited for him to prop himself up on his elbow before passing him the glass. He choked, swallowing them, coughing as he naturally tried to dislodge the intrusion from his throat. "Take another drink," I encouraged, rubbing his back when he did.

The room was warm, and we'd been under the covers too. Before he could pull them to his throat again, I stripped them off the bed, leaving only a sheet and turned on the aircon. Whispering into the phone, I ordered a green tea with lemon and honey from room service and dressed in a pair of boxer shorts to wait for them. I'd barely replaced the cold compress on Scottie's forehead when the soft knock at the door sounded. The pot was still steaming as I poured Scottie a cup and doctored it. He cringed when he sipped it, only managing half before he collapsed, falling into a restless sleep again. Tossing and turning, he alternated between shivering and stripping off the sheet covering him. I replaced the cold compress over and over again, waiting for his fever to break, but it didn't look like it would happen any time soon. The glands in his throat were swollen, detectable from the lightest touch, so his snoring didn't come as a surprise, but I knew the sore throat would make it worse.

The alarm went off just before dawn, but I reset it to give him a couple more hours' sleep. I needed Scottie's help hooking up the float, loading the bulls, and getting out of the showgrounds. Once we were on the road, I could handle it, but the close quarters manoeuvring necessary to get our quarry onboard was something entirely out of my depth.

Dawn lit the sky, and the brilliant blue of winter in south-east Queensland slowly appeared. Scottie groaned and rolled over, his hand pressed to his forehead. "I feel like death warmed up. What happened?"

"You're sick." I pressed my hand to his face. He was still clammy, but thankfully, the medicine and cold compresses were working—his fever was down. "You're nearly due for some more paracetamol, but you can have ibuprofen now to help your throat. Let's get you another cuppa and some brekkie so I can dose you up, then we can get on the road to the showgrounds."

"Yeah, okay," he muttered, still rubbing his head.

His movements were slow. Pained. And I was powerless to make things better. We hadn't passed any pharmacies on our way here from the showgrounds, but I'd googled it and knew there was an all-night one around the corner. I packed our things and dropped our bags down to the four-by-four as Scottie showered. When I returned, he was more alert but still looked like death warmed up, his skin a pallid grey as he slipped on his boots.

"Let's get out of here, hey?" I grasped his elbow, helping to guide him down to the lobby before I checked out and getting us loaded into the Landcruiser as gently as I could. I detoured to the strip shopping centre, ordering breakfast at the café next door to the chemist before ducking in there and picking up a collection of over-the-counter medicine—cough drops, pain killers, cold and flu tablets, and jelly beans, because they were a must-have sick food. Our scrambled eggs and bacon, freshly squeezed juice and our cuppas were ready by the time I headed back there. Juggling everything, I passed Scottie his breakfast, cup of tea, and the cold and flu tablets before going around to the driver's side and eating my fill. We needed to get on the road, and as the streets filled with morning commuters, I realized my mistake. I'd let Scottie sleep in, but now I'd have to navigate peak hour traffic with a float.

"You'll be right," Scottie croaked, and so began our nightmare journey back home.

TEN

Scottie

had no idea what was wrong when I'd woken, but as I'd come to long enough to swallow and try to lift my head from the pillow, it became obvious. The Ekka was held only a couple of weeks before the start of spring, but it was peak flu season. I usually managed to catch a sniffle, but I'd never felt this bad before. And it only got worse. Where I'd managed most of the drive down, all I could do when we got to the showgrounds was hook up our trailer and get it positioned near the cattle run we were using to load the bulls on. Dizziness overwhelmed me as I stepped out of the vehicle. If it wasn't for Pete standing next to me, I'd have fallen on my arse. He bundled me into the back seat with a rolled-up jacket, instructing me to use it as a pillow and sleep. I barely heard his explanation to the bloke standing next to us, catching only the comment that I wasn't drunk but sick. When I stirred next, we were on the road, but it wasn't the one I expected to be on. We shouldn't have been anywhere near Australia Zoo, but the first thing I saw when I blinked open my eyes was a picture of Steve Irwin at the turnoff for the road named after him. Pete was taking us the long way, up the coast road, then west out to Longreach and south-west to the station. It'd add a few hundred kilo-metres to the trip and a few hours driving.

"Why?" I croaked—

"Oh, thank God," he huffed. "I've been looking over my shoulder trying to see if you're okay but couldn't see your face properly. How're you feeling?"

"Okay?" Maybe. Truth was, my head was pounding, every muscle ached, and in the minute I'd been awake, I'd been both hot and cold. "Why are we going this way?"

"Because I'm not stupid enough to attempt Cunning-ham's Gap with a few tonne of bulls and float attached to the back of the car." It made sense. The Gap was treacher-ous. A steep road switched back on itself—with hairpin turns at every point—connected the city to the east and ru-ral western Queensland on the other side. Travelling west, we'd be going up the range carrying the weight of the trailer and the cattle. It was a challenge. Even experienced truckies had trouble going through the Gap, burning brakes or gears, and crashing off the roads. Mostly they stopped in the run-off lanes built to bring heavy vehicles to a quick stop with-out sending them plunging off the steep edges, but it wasn't unheard of for trucks to stall on the steep uphill runs and roll backwards. Fatalities happened there, and even more injuries. Pete was playing it safe, and I appreciated his cau-tion.

"Thank you," I rasped. "I'd still be dying in the hotel room if it weren't for you."

"I'm glad I was here," He reached back and rubbed a hand over my knee, and I grasped his hand, squeezing it. "You're really warm, Scottie. Take your jumper off?"

I did and followed it up with a swig of water from the bottle Pete passed back to me. "Need me to drive for a bit?" I asked.

"Nah, I've got this. You sit back and relax. Lie down again and take another nap if you feel like it."

"Wouldn't mind moving into the front seat actually. Feeling a bit better now."

"Okay, no worries. As soon as we get to the next exit or rest stop, I'll pull off." It was only ten minutes later that I was wobbling like a newborn calf as I stepped out of the back and heaved myself into the front already out of breath. I hid my shaking hands, busying myself with the settings on the radio. Soon we had the soft strains of a guitar twanging over the speakers, and only a moment later, Pete's phone buzzed through the hands-free system. "Hey, Ma," he greeted.

"How are you doing, love? You coping with the float? Is Scottie okay?"

"Yeah, I'm doing great. Scottie's awake too." He glanced sideways at me and pressed a hand to my forehead. "He's hot, shivering as well, even though he's trying to hide it, and he's weak, but at least he's awake."

I sputtered out an objection, but I lost my credibility when the sputter turned into a cough that made me sound like I'd been a pack-a-day smoker for half my life. Pete rubbed my back as I rested my elbows on my knees, trying not to pass out from the dizziness. As soon as I'd composed myself enough, he handed me the water bottle and popped a cough lozenge for me. Sometime during my coughing fit, he'd said bye to Ma and was concentrating on both driving and making me feel human enough to sit upright. My eyes were heavy again and my body ached as my energy levels were sucked desperately low from the hacking cough.

"Sleep, babe," he whispered as I closed my eyes.

Confusion reigned supreme. I should have been scared, but I was floating, drifting on the warm currents that the eagles soared on. I heard a voice. Warm and calming. I knew him. But had I dreamed him? Or was he real? I didn't think I could fly, but there I was, blue surrounding me everywhere. Alone. I looked around, trying to find him. Trying to see the person attached to the voice, but all I could hear was babble and a beeping that seemed to pass through me, making everything, including my teeth, ache as it went off.

I wanted the voice again. Strained to hear him. Then he spoke and I could breathe. I relaxed, swooping and flying through the loops on a rollercoaster. I listened to his voice, trying to understand what he was saying. But I couldn't. The words didn't make any sense. It was as if he was speaking another language. But I recognized the panic in his words. Then I was falling. Getting tossed around, spinning like a falling leaf. I didn't hit the ground, but I knew I was on it.

The sky changed colour. Red clouds gathered, and unfamiliar voices were close by, but I couldn't see them. Fear pulsed through me. I pulled away, trying to run. I was being chased. My heart hammered in my chest, and I tried to shield myself from the attack. Then a steady hand reached out, gently gripping my arm, guiding it down by my side again. "Shh, Scottie. It's okay," the voice said. I understood the words. I knew him. I loved him. I wanted to sink into the feeling he gave me—warmth and safety. I tried to move towards him, but the hand shifted, pulling away. I cried out, my brain unable to turn feelings into words.

I was rudderless again, this time in choppy seas. Waves crashed over me, and I was drowning in the storm. I reached out for him, wishing he could save me. The same touch came, this time on my chest, gently pushing me down. But instead of pushing me under, the water was draining away, and I could breathe once more. I slumped back, taking a lungful of oxygen, but the world around me changed again. Bright light burned my eyes, and I tried to turn away, to shield my vision from the blinding rays. I was falling, tumbling down a mountainside catching on trees and bouncing off them like I was in a pinball machine. Scrambling to hold onto something, I latched onto the voice again. My mind was a jumbled mess, much like the mass of weeds and vines I was getting tangled in, stopping my fall. I tried again to open my eyes, but I couldn't. The light hurt too much. It pierced through the thick canopy, blinding me.

Why were people poking and prodding me? I coughed again, and a giant picked me up, plucking me from the tangle of vines. He squeezed and my lungs seized, crushing my chest. He shook me, tossing my body around like I was a rag doll. Where was I? What was I?

Another voice spoke and I recognized her too. When I heard them speak, I knew I was safe. The darkness came again, and I welcomed it, sinking into rest as the hand keeping me safe never left my chest. Its weight was a comfort.

When I woke, there were no lights, but the beeping remained. I breathed in slowly, my chest tight, and every muscle aching like I'd run with the bulls and lost. Something tickled my arm and I reached out, touching it gently. A person. I ran my fingers through that hair I knew. I thought about where I'd been. It was all confused, but I knew Pete was with me the whole time. I'd heard him.

I remembered Steve Irwin too, but I didn't know why.

"Welcome back," Ma whispered, and I turned my head towards the sound. In the dim light, I made out her silhouette. "You had us all worried sick, hon."

"Where am I?" I croaked.

"Longreach Hospital. Pete drove straight through from Brisbane. You slept most of the way, but your fever spiked again in the late afternoon when he was in-between towns. He did what he could, but by the time he got to Jericho, you were delirious. The servo owner told him that there was no doc close by, and the hospitals were either back in Emerald or Longreach. He was halfway between the two, so he forged on ahead. The ER docs admitted you immediately and put you on an IV to rehydrate you. You've been in and out of consciousness since. They've run some tests and we're waiting on the results, but it looks like a nasty strain of influenza—"

"I have the flu? That's it?" I groaned and shook my head. I tried to prop myself up a little, but the canular in my hand pinched, and I hissed. "Damn it, get this thing outta me. I'm fine to go home."

"No, you're not," Pete mumbled, wrapping an arm around my waist and nuzzling my leg, still fast asleep.

"Listen to your man, Scottie. He knows best." I huffed and rolled my eyes before Ma spoke again. "You left Brisbane two days ago. One day driving, the other hooked up to every kind of machine monitoring you as other machines fed you on a drip. You were talking, but none of it made sense. Thrashing around in the bed too. Then Pete would speak, and you'd reach out for him. He'd touch you and you'd instantly calm. He hasn't left your side once."

I reached down and ran my fingers through his hair, touching his temple and brushing his scruffy jaw with the backs of my fingers. "I'm sorry, babe," I whispered. "Ma," I breathed, not able to put into words what I wanted to say.

"You concentrate on getting better." She patted my hand, and Pete nuzzled my leg, from his spot hunched over on the chair. "I'll try and persuade Pete to check into a motel so he can get a good night's sleep. He refused point-blank to come back to the station unless it was with you."

"What about the bulls?" I asked, although I needn't have bothered. If it wasn't Ma or Ally who took over, Jono would have made sure they were okay.

"Jono dropped me off. He swapped the float to the ute and drove the cattle home. Left the Landcruiser here for us."

Pete stirred and raised his head, blinking a few times as he focussed on me. He cupped my jaw in his hands and shifted so he was sitting on the edge of the bed. "I think I might go and grab a cuppa. Excuse me for half an hour or so, boys." I loved Ma and appreciated everything she did, but none more so than giving Pete and me a few moments alone.

"You're awake," he whispered, brushing his thumbs over my cheeks. Infinitely gentle. He leaned in and kissed my forehead, barely a brush of his lips, but the fog of my medicated sleep lifted, and the love he shared spread through me like a springtime breeze, warming every part of my soul. We hadn't said the words. We didn't need to—actions had always been more important to me—but I knew Pete was in as deep as me.

"You've been here the whole time," I croaked, my voice rough from the coughing I must have been doing.

"I have. They wanted me to leave, but Ma sorted it out so I could stay." He gave me a small smile and pressed another kiss to my forehead. "How are you feeling?"

"Kinda floaty. Not quite with it. Tired too." I yawned, my eyes slipping closed again. "Why am I so tired?"

"Because your body has been through hell these last couple of days. Sleep, Scottie. I'll be right here the whole time."

"You need sleep too," I mumbled.

"I'm fine. Don't worry about me."

I spent another twenty-four hours in hospital. I was itching to get out of there. Although I'd insisted that I could walk, apparently it was hospital policy to walk you out in a wheelchair. So, my busting through the front doors was a lot slower than I'd fantasized about while I was stuck in bed, but it was just as good. I tilted my face up to the mid-morning sun and closed my eyes, letting its warmth seep into me. Pete pulled up in the Landcruiser, and Ma held the wheelchair steady as I gingerly lifted myself out and stepped on still-unsteady legs into the back seat. I only remembered the first hour or so of the drive back to the station before waking up again outside of the homestead. Ally followed me into the loungeroom as Pete and Jono helped me sit down.

"You need anything?" she asked, a little hesitantly.

"Nah, I'm okay. Just tired." I coughed again, the rattle in my chest shaking me to my core. By the time I stopped coughing, tears were running down my face. Pete had a glass of water ready for me to take a drink from, and Ally was white as a ghost.

"I watched the news last night," she murmured. "A thirty-five-year-old lady died of influenza yesterday. Over three hundred people just this year."

"Oh Ally," Pete murmured, wrapping her in his arms. She buried her head in his chest and fisted his shirt before taking a breath and pulling back. Her eyes were glassy, like she'd been blinking back tears, and she pointed to me.

"You die, Scottie, and I'll fucking kill you." I grinned at her and held out my hand. When she took it, she added, "And if I get sick, I'll make your life bloody miserable."

"I'm fine, Ally. It knocked me round pretty bad, but I'm feeling a hundred percent better than I was yesterday. I'm not gonna die." I looked at Pete, making the same promise to him as Ally. "No way."

Two weeks had passed since my stint in hospital, and I was finally back on light duties, which literally meant taking vegetable scraps out to the chickens, collecting the eggs, letting the horses out—but God forbid that I even attempt to muck out their stalls—and when I hadn't been coughing too much, watering Nan's veggie patch. I was getting sick of everyone hovering, and frustrated at not having anything to do, but I knew it was out of love. And necessity. I wanted to do more, but if I pushed too hard, I ended up exhausted and sleeping the day away. It was the only reason I hadn't lost my shit and headed off for a ride on Tilly.

Now we had more than one person sick and I was worried. Pete and I went to the Ekka and brought home a bug that we really could have done without. Yindi and I hadn't had much contact, but it was enough. She'd gone down like a ton of bricks, and with two of us out sick, it'd been all hands on deck. The cows' gestation periods were advancing, and a couple had run into problems, but Jono seemed to have that under control with Ally, Craig, and Sam's help. We'd had a dingo attack the chicken coop, tearing the gate off its hinges and killing half a dozen of our birds, including Hinchey. Surprisingly, we'd found the others around the homestead stressed and dazed rather than dead and eaten. Den had spent the better part of a day rebuilding the coop to make it as predator-proof as possible and had then reinforced the fly screens in all the living quarters to make sure we were in predator-proof housing too.

Then there was the wombat.

I was watching Pete with it now. He'd heard noises a few weeks earlier and seen one disappear under the guesthouse. He hadn't thought much of it until we returned, when we'd both heard the snuffling and grunting. He'd shone the torchlight under the guesthouse in the middle of the night and disturbed a very grumpy, very pregnant mamma about to enter her burrow. There was no way she could stay there. Wombat burrows could be thirty-metres long and would destabilize the foundations of the house if built underneath one of the stumps, or do some serious damage to the plumbing if the pipes got in its way. So, Pete being Pete hadn't come back to bed. Instead, he'd researched what to do, finding that they needed to be able to get out from underneath the structure but not back in. He'd closed in the openings the wombat could fit through, and to stop it from digging under the siding of the old Queenslander, he'd dug a trench around the guesthouse a good foot deep, strung out chicken wire along it and backfilled the area. Then he'd done the same to the homestead. I'd tried helping him. All of us had, but he'd flat-out refused, insisting it was something he was perfectly capable of fixing. I knew he felt useless, not wanting to go too far away from me in case I needed him, but also needing to contribute something. Making matters worse, we still hadn't been back to Quilpie to collect his metal detector. We'd planned on getting it on our way back through, but circumstances and all that. As soon as I was allowed to venture out of Ma's sight for the day, we'd be going to pick it up.

Until then, I was watching my man implement step three of his grand plan to relocate mumma wombat—lure her out with fresh vegetables and grass, trap her in the carry box Den had whipped up and move her to the burrow he'd found in one of the paddocks. Arse sticking up as he shuffled back, dropping the grassy tops off the carrots, pieces of pumpkin and clumps of native grass that he'd pulled from the water troughs in the horse paddock, I got to watch his arse wiggle enticingly. I also had to discreetly adjust myself under the bulky hoodie I was wearing because the one thing worse than being sick was also being sex-starved. Pete hadn't laid a hand on me for far too long, arguing that I was exhausted and needed to preserve my energy. He was right, but I wanted to taste him so badly I was nearly at bursting point.

"That boy has a fine arse, doesn't he?" Nan murmured from her spot next to me on the swing, before dabbing her nose with a hankie.

I snorted out a laugh, coughing once into my cup of tea. "He does," I agreed, still grinning.

"Perfect handful," she observed, side-eyeing me and no doubt waiting to see if I'd take the bait and get embarrassed or tell her to stop.

"You can try to get a rise outta me, Nan, but I'm not gonna bite."

This time it was Nan's turn to laugh. It came out as more of a gasping laugh. She sounded like she was having trouble breathing. "How long have you been feelin' under the weather?" Nan had been pushing herself, looking after more than her usual cooking and cleaning. It gave Ma some spare time to look after me and Yindi when Waru needed help, as well as keep on top of the paperwork and contract negotiations for IGA, but she was doing too much.

Mark had partly come through for us, IGA increasing our rates per head of cattle. But they'd also reduced the term of the contract, wanting some ability to drop the rate back if the troughs weren't built. But we needed certainty. A longer contract was critical—we needed to know where our income was coming from and the number of head we needed to produce so we could properly budget. We'd be up shit creek if we invested the kind of cash we wanted to into the water tank project without having security of supply terms. So, Ma had been on conference call after conference call with their lawyers and ours trying to nut out terms that were satisfactory to all. We were slowly seeing progress, but I wouldn't be counting my chickens, so to speak, until I had the amended contract in front of me. "Nan, we've been sick as dogs. You've got to take it easier."

"I'm fine, Scottie. It's just a winter cold."

"Yeah, when I've had influenza and Yindi came down sick while I was still contagious. Nan, we need you healthy."

"Nan, don't screw around with this," Ally added from behind me. I didn't even realize she was standing there, and I jumped when she spoke. Shock made my heart rate spike and my steaming cuppa spill over my hand. I hissed and swapped hands, shaking off the hot tea from the other. "If you're not feeling a hundred percent, you need to be resting." Ally paused for a moment and added, "What the hell is he doing?"

"Stage three of his grand plan to relocate the wombat. If he can get it in the box, it'll be a bloody miracle, but if he does, he's got a good chance of pulling off the relocation. Apparently, wombats move into other disused burrows all the time. I'm just hoping the one Pete found hasn't become a snake's den. But let's not change the subject. Nan, listen to Ally."

"You've been moaning about getting back to work since you arrived home." Nan pointed out, and I laughed.

"I might've been moaning about getting back to work, but doing anything more than moving from my bed to the couch wiped me out for hours when I first got sick. Even now, I sleep for a few hours in the afternoon because collecting the eggs and watering your veggie patch wipes me out."

Nan coughed, and the sound startled both me and Ally. Ally jumped forwards to rub Nan's back, and I went for her tea so she didn't spill it and scald herself.

"Scottie—" Pete started, his face full of concern, even as he rubbed the back of his head. He'd scrambled up and was jogging over to us when I pointed to Nan, making him stop in his tracks, turn on a dime and yell out to Ma in the stable.

Ma appeared out of breath next to us a moment later and took over, ordering Nan inside out of the cool breeze and onto her recliner. She refilled her cuppa and checked her temperature, sorting out some paracetamol when she discovered it was in raging fever range. Ally brought over a wet facecloth and placed it on her forehead. Speaking to me, Ma ordered, "You stay close to Nan and keep an eye on her. I'll go finish up and—"

"I'll do it, Ma," Pete interjected. They conversed for a moment, and Pete took off outside, taking over whatever Ma was doing in the barn, the wombat forgotten for the moment.

"I'm getting the doc out here," Ma decided, hovering over Nan and touching the backs of her fingers to Nan's cheek. When Nan pushed her off, tutting at her, Ma turned her gaze on Nan. "If Scottie is anything to go by, by the time the doc gets here, you'll need him urgently. And Yindi isn't doing too great either."

"Not necessary," Nan huffed from her spot on the lounge. But even as she said it, she laid her head back on the recliner and closed her eyes. She looked every one of her years, and it terrified me knowing that our tough-as-nails nan was already frail and would get worse. I met Ma's gaze and nodded. It'd knocked me around enough to be scary. But Nan was decades older than me, and we weren't going to lose her through stubbornness.

ELEVEN

Pete

Two bloody days. I couldn't believe it. We'd called the doc two bloody days ago. I was expecting a visit that night or the next morning, not waiting for two bloody days with still no sign of him. Yindi was getting better. She'd pushed through and was regaining her strength. She'd be fine provided she didn't get a secondary infection. But Nan was scaring us all half to death. She'd barely been out of bed since she fell sick and she was still there. Ma had swapped shifts with Ally hours earlier, swabbing down her forehead, trying to keep her cool. Scottie had taken a cuppa into her at nine and cried in my arms when he'd walked out. She'd aged a decade overnight and was frailer than he'd ever seen her.

Nan now needed help lifting her cup of tea, and when she relaxed into her pillows, she seemed to sink into them, folding in on herself. Her skin, a pallid grey, was almost translucent, the blue veins showing clearly against her gnarled hands, hands that had been less bony and less clawed only the day before. She stopped insisting she was fine, and Scottie and I shared a look, his one of devastation and mine trying to convince him her illness wasn't his fault. Her whimper when she shifted had Scottie jumping up to aid her, and my heart broke. My worst fears for this family crystalized. If they lost her... Scottie wouldn't be able to live with himself.

Nan's cough rattled in her chest, and she became weaker as the hours waiting for the doctor passed. When she started referring to Scottie as Henry—apparently Pop's name—and asking when they were leaving for the muster, Ma kicked into action, ordering Ally to pack an overnight bag while she called ahead to the ER in Longreach Hospital. She told Scottie to get the car, but I stepped in. "No, I'll get it. You stay with Nan." If she thought Scottie was her husband, he needed to stay with her. I'd seen how scared and upset Scottie was when he'd been sick and hallucinating. He hadn't understood what was happening. At least if he stayed here with her, she'd have people around her that she knew and felt safe around. There was no way I would risk Nan feeling alone and afraid.

I ran to the shed, my heart thudding against my chest as nerves and fear swirled in my gut. They had a long drive ahead of them, and those hours would be critical. I refused to think of what would happen if they didn't get to the hospital in time. I brought the car around and skidded to a halt in front of the house, immediately making for the stairs. But another cloud of dust on the drive in the distance caught my attention. Still a good minute away, I paused. The only person we were expecting was the doc. Could it really be him?

"Ally," I yelled. "Ma, I think the doc's coming." I was up the stairs to the front door, yanking it open as Ally pushed through, and the relief that swept over her made tears spring to her eyes. She covered her mouth and smothered a sob as I wrapped an arm around her. "Come on, Al, let's go meet him."

The doc pulled up, and he retrieved a black bag out of the boot of his car before striding up to meet us. Greying and with a belly that hinted at a few too many beers, he was dressed in grey slacks and a light blue button-up shirt. "Ally," he greeted warmly. "How's our patient?"

"Not great." Ally stepped out of the way, and I held open the door open for her and the doc. I was glad he'd dispensed with excessive pleasantries, because I might have lost my shit if he'd stayed outside and chatted. "She's mistaking Scottie for Pop. We haven't been able to get her fever down, and she's barely drinking anything so we're pretty sure she's dehydrated."

"Right. Let's do an assessment then." He got down to business, asking Nan all sorts of questions. She had trouble answering most of them. She didn't even have a clue what year it was. Watching Scottie's delirious ramblings had made me think he was scared, maybe anxious, and he'd told me about being chased, falling, and floating. But Nan was totally different. She seemed to go back in time, getting everyone mixed up with characters from her past. The doc checked her vitals and blew out a breath. "Okay, I can't be certain enough to start any treatments until we run a blood test, but managing her symptoms has reached critical level. Karen needs to be hospitalized. You've done all the right things, so if this was an ordinary cold, she'd likely not have come down as ill as she is. With Scott having had influenza, there's a good chance that's what she has."

I blew out a breath, fighting to keep the panic at bay and watching Scottie's reaction. He was blaming himself, and no matter what any of us said, he'd continue to do so. I'd read enough news reports to know that this year's influenza strain was vicious, and elderly people were struggling against it, and losing. The next few days would make all the difference—either Nan would pull through, or this family would change irrevocably.

Time seemed to drag. The four-hour trip to Longreach lasted a month. Every bump in the road like a mountain to traverse. Every curve, the length of the great Australian bite. I drove, Scottie beside me, holding my hand, and Ally in the back. Nan and Ma were in the doc's car so he could keep an eye on her.

Then there was the waiting at the hospital. It was eternal. Nan was taken straight through to ER, the doctor on duty seeing her as soon as she arrived. But Scottie, Ally, and I sat in the uncomfortable chairs in the waiting room. Rows of plastic seats, attached with a shared armrest, ran along the perimeter of the room. A tele flashed up today's news bulletins from the free to air channel. And we waited.

Ma came out a few hours later looked haggard. She rubbed her temples and spoke quietly. "They're transferring Nan out of ER and into an isolation unit. The test came back positive for influenza."

"Is she stabilizing?" I asked, wrapping my arm around Scottie's shoulders. He'd barely said a word since we'd left.

Since the doctor confirmed his beloved nan needed to be hospitalized. Scottie leaned closer and I squeezed his shoulder, giving him as much comfort as I could in the confines of a public waiting room. He'd been approached by at least three different people who were checking up on Nan; Scottie was right—news travelled fast in the country town.

Ma shook her head and held her hands out. "I have no idea. The nurses tell me it's too soon to really have made a difference. Her fever is lower, but her breathing is no better, and her cough sounds even worse in this air-conditioning. They're pumping her full of antivirals, so hopefully, that will start to kick in soon."

Hours waiting turned into days. We were kicked out of the waiting room that first night at the end of visiting hours, but Ma stayed on. We took her dinner and checked into the same motel I'd stayed at, crashing on the bed as soon as we arrived. Ally insisted on swapping with Ma overnight so she could get some rest. Scottie wanted to be there too, but she forced him to get some sleep. I'd agreed. As much as he wanted to be with her, the last thing we all needed was Scottie getting a secondary infection because he'd pushed himself too hard.

"Come on," I'd said. "You need to rest. You're no good to Nan if you get sick again."

Scottie pulled me into his arms and sighed, burying his face in my chest. "I wanna sleep for a week," he groaned when we finally laid down.

"Sleep, Scottie." I ran my fingers through his hair, the silky-soft strands tickling my skin. It was those quiet moments, just the two of us, that reinforced just how perfect life with Scottie was. While everything teetered on the edge of uncertainty—tonight would be critical for Nan—those stolen moments we had were the ones that recharged our souls. His breathing deepened and I thought he was on the brink of falling asleep when he spoke again.

"What if she doesn't make it, babe?" His words were pained, terrified. I held him tighter, trying to soothe his aching heart through my touch.

"We face it together. All of us." I couldn't promise him that Nan would be fine, not when I'd seen him so sick and for so long, but I couldn't let him give up hope either. "We'll be there for her helping every step of the way."

I woke to an empty bed, but Scottie wasn't far. Standing at the window, wearing only the faded jeans he'd worn the day before, feet bare against the linoleum floor, I watched him check the screen, black it out again only to check it again a moment later. When it buzzed, he jumped and scrambled not to drop it, swiping it open and reading the message. He breathed out and closed his eyes, resting his hands on the windowsill and letting his head fall against the glass. "How's Nan?"

He jumped before laughing. "She's better. Stronger." He smiled radiantly. The shadows lingering in his eyes lightened, his back straightening.

"Good. That's good." I rose and staggered my way over to him, my body screaming for a good dose of caffeine. "How about we pick up a couple of clean shirts for us, even if they're just from the servo, then get some breakfast and take it into the hospital for Ally. We can relieve her for a while and sit with Nan. Give her a chance to sleep, and Ma a moment to get a change of clothes for them."

"Sounds like a plan." So that's what we did. By the time lunch rolled around, Ma had arrived to relieve Scottie and me, and Nan was sleeping peacefully. She'd managed a few sips of the chicken broth but had been sucking on ice the whole morning. Combined with the IV fluids she was receiving, the nurses were satisfied she was getting enough.

A knock at the door had me lifting my head. Scottie blinked his eyes awake from his post leaning against the wall, and Ma turned towards the door. A priest stood there, dressed in black pants and a shirt, with a while collar. Holding a briefcase, he smiled at Ma and nodded at Scottie and me. "Mind if I come and visit for a while?"

Nan began coughing, and all attention turned to her. Her eyes were open, and one hand covered her mouth, the other pointing at the priest. "What are you doing here?" she cried. "No!" Alarm radiated off Ma, and she instantly shifted, grasping Nan's hand. Scottie moved to her other side and closed his hand around her wrist, lending her comfort. I jumped up too, torn between physically throwing the priest out of the room and calming Nan. I found myself moving, standing at the foot of Nan's bed, watching helplessly as she shifted, gritting her teeth. "It's not my time yet," she ground out. "I'm not that bloody sick. Fairdinkum, you'd better not be reading me my last rights."

I froze and my grip loosened from around the metal guard on the bed. A bark of laughter sounded from Ma, a strangled kind of sob-snort that sounded almost crazed. "You silly old woman, he's not reading you your last rights. He's coming to say g'day."

I held my breath, trying to calm my racing heart. There was movement next to me and hands were on my shoulders, cupping them, calming me. Scottie. He slid his hands down my arms and closed his hands around my clenched fists, tugging them away from the bar. "It's okay," he whispered for my ears only. "Just breathe."

"Truly I'm not." The priest smiled at her, before glancing at Scottie and me. His eyes lingered and Scottie pulled away, letting go of me like I'd singed him.

Shame crawled over me like a hundred spiders clambering over my skin. It stole my breath and turned my stomach. My voice was rough like sandpaper. "I'll wait outside. I shouldn't even be in here."

I strode out, barely resisting the urge to run as I followed the long hallway to the entrance of the hospital. I pushed through the double doors wishing that I could shuck off the embarrassment and shame that swamped me. Spring air swirled around me. Dry and dusty and so much warmer than only a few weeks ago. We'd already hit average temperatures equivalent to Sydney's summer, and we were still only a couple of weeks into spring.

"Hey, everything okay?" Ally asked as she stepped up next to me after I'd been standing there for what felt like an age.

"Nan's fine," I mumbled.

"And you?" Ally asked, concern creasing her forehead. "Are you okay?"

I huffed. "Not really, no." Then I shook my head. I had no reason to be upset. None whatsoever. No right. We'd agreed that we'd keep our relationship on the down-low. Scottie had reached out for me, touched me in front of their damn priest. What did I expect? That his hands would linger longer than they did? That he'd wrap me up? I was going out of my mind. Seeing him sick had shaken me to my core. The inner strength he displayed was still there. That iron will to survive and succeed against all the odds. He'd turned it inwards, fighting the virus inside him. He was still the same person, the same man I'd fallen for. And we were in exactly the same position we'd been in only a few weeks ago— deeply closeted. I shook off the melancholy and squared my shoulders. "I'm okay. Let some stuff in my head get to me, but I'm all right now."

"You sure?" she asked, looking as if she didn't really believe me.

I smiled, reminding myself that it didn't matter if the world had no idea about us. The important people knew— Scottie's family. He was open with them. No one else mattered. "Yeah. Yeah, I'm sure. It's hard sometimes when I forget we have to hide. I'm not used to doing that, but I know we need to."

"You're out in Sydney, aren't you?" It was a rhetorical question, but I answered anyway.

"I was. I've marched in every pride parade since I was a teenager and been to Mardi Gras for four years running. But he's worth it. I'd give up—I have given up—all those things in a heartbeat to have him, and I don't regret any of it." I shook my head and jammed my hands in my pockets, the green tee with Longreach written in bold letters across the front of it, stretching across my shoulders as I hunched them. "I just wish it didn't sting so much when he recoiled from me. I don't know what I was expecting. It's not as if we can be open in front of the priest."

Ally shook her head, looking sad. "Yeah, I can see why Scottie recoiled. Father McPherson's predecessor was very vocal about 'the gays'." She curled her index and middle fingers over, mimicking quotation marks as she said the last couple of words. "Scottie stopped going to church after that sermon."

We stood outside for another few minutes talking, until Ally motioned inside. "I should go."

"Yeah, I don't want to overwhelm Nan. Too many visitors, you know. I'll wait out here." She smiled sadly at me, pressing her lips together and nodding slowly before she entered. I watched her go inside, wishing that Scottie would appear in her place. When he came out, it only took him a moment to spot me sitting on the park bench in the gardens.

"I wasn't sure you'd still be here," he murmured as he eased himself down next to me. "But I couldn't get out of there without being rude to Father McPherson. He kept asking me about the station and how things were going, and all I wanted to do was escape and come find you."

"I'm an idiot. I shouldn't have run out. I'm not angry or upset with you. I just needed some air." I gave him a small smile. "I know we can't be open and I'm totally okay with that, but it still stings when we have to jump apart."

"I'm sorry," he breathed, hands clasped between his bent knees and head hanging low. "I don't mean to hurt you."

I wanted to reach out for him, but I knocked my knee gently into his instead. "You don't hurt me. Not intentionally, and I know that these insecurities I have are just that. It's not that you don't want me, or that you're ashamed. You have a real need. I get that and I don't want you to risk everything for me. I just need to get used to it."

"I don't want to force you to do anything you don't want to do. You shouldn't have to go back in the closet for me. I hate that you're doing this."

"I don't. Because I get to have you, and you're worth it." Scottie leaned into me and knocked me with his shoulder, lingering closer. Our gazes met and held, and he smiled softly, the affection lingering in his eyes stealing my breath.

Nan was in hospital for a week, and Ma and Ally stayed there, one of them sitting with her at all times. Scottie and I headed back to the station after the second night, not wanting to leave the hands to fend for themselves any longer than necessary. I was starting to appreciate the new

Hinchy's wake-up calls first thing in the morning. The damn rooster made sure we were all awake at the arse crack of dawn, and it gave me a chance to get out and collect the eggs, dropping them back to Scottie for him to start breakfast and get the pot of tea on while I completed his morning jobs for him. We worked as a team, the two of us cooking and cleaning and keeping a handle on the everyday jobs. Scottie was getting stronger every day. He'd stopped needing afternoon naps and he seemed more himself, his energy levels returning and shaking off the grumpiness.

When we finally got the call to pick up Nan, Ma, and Ally, Jono offered to go, telling us to head in the opposite direction and collect my metal detector. The shop had called again, telling me to hurry up and collect it or he'd sell it. Thankfully, it was a minor fix; one busted wire from landing on it as I'd tried to scramble away from the snake.

The temptation to go out there and start searching again was there, but it was hard too. The disappointment had shredded me, made me question the worth of all the years and money I'd sunk into chasing down every possible rumour and piece of slightly more reliable evidence, and some that were crack-pot conspiracy theories. If I never went out again, never disproved my theory, I'd never be disappointed. Of course, I didn't share any of this with Scottie. If I had, he'd drive me straight out to the reef and insist that we stay until we found gold. But he had other things to worry about. His family needed him, and with Yindi and Scottie on much lighter duties, and Ma and Ally looking after Nan full-time, we both needed to help out around the station. It'd be stupidly selfish of me to try to get out to the reef anytime before Nan was 100 percent.

We pulled up to the homestead just after the others, and it was all hands on deck getting Nan settled back in and dinner cooked.

Nan was weak—much weaker than Scottie had been after his stay in hospital—but she was getting better. At two months post her release, she still needed Ma and Ally's help with a few things, and we tried to lighten their load so they could be there for her. Scottie had started taking back some of his morning chores, but I still did most of the heavy lifting when it came to mucking out the stables and the chicken coop. There were no more dingo attacks and I hadn't heard anything more from the wombat, but the guesthouse was lying vacant. No one even seemed to notice where I was at night, and I was counting on that to continue. With so much work to do and so few bodies on the ground, we'd all just pitched in. Exhausted smiles were traded at each meal, and everyone quickly retired to their quarters. My cleaning up afterwards had become the norm. On the weekends that the stockmen would normally go into Longreach, everyone stayed home, spending their time catching up on sleep and hanging out around the small campfire we lit by the homestead.

Now that things had started getting back to normal, it was right in time for calving. Instead of finally settling back in and taking it easy, the real work was about to start. Calving was complicated. Rationally I understood it. I knew that there would be orphaned calves and cows who lost their young. But seeing it was a totally different thing. The first few calves that were born seemed to go smoothly. They were suckling well, and it was happy times. They were awfully cute too—all knobbly knees and fluffy hair. But then Mabel was born.

Scottie and I were patrolling the mob on our four-wheelers, puttering around the herd, and making sure there was enough noise and light to deter any dingoes that might fancy a newborn calf for dinner. When Scottie spotted something and pulled away from me, heading for a particular cow, I doubled back, looping around and following him in. He was on the radio when I got there, calling out Jono to start the next shift early. "Stay with me until Jono and Den get here, then I need you to keep patrolling. Dotty's in distress. Something isn't right. I need to check her over."

"Can I help?"

He gave me rapid-fire instructions as he felt around the cow's mid-section, shaking his head as she laid down. "Damn it," he muttered. "I think the calf is breached. We'll lose both if I can't get it out. She's weakening already." He looked around, headlights nowhere to be seen. "Get Jono on the radio again. Find out what's taking so long for them to get here."

I did, but there was no response, headlights appearing in the distance instead. "Over there, Scottie." I pointed, and he followed my gaze, continuing to feel around the cow's stomach.

"Keep her calm. Stay out the way of her legs. She likes her head being scratched between her ears. Just keep talking to her. This is gonna hurt." I did what he asked, scratching her head and running my hand over her hair. I murmured to her, soft and slow, trying to calm her as her eyes widened and her moo sounded like a horse's whinny. Scottie had his arm buried in her, feeling around and trying to reposition the calf. Wheels skidded nearby and Jono and Den came running, their headlights illuminating the area where Scottie was working. I leaned down closer, cuddling the cow's head and stroking her hair. She was pulling against me, not fighting my hold, but whining as Scottie pulled and cursed. Jono dropped immediately to his knees, manipulating the calf from outside her belly as Scottie pushed and pulled from inside, the whole time telling Dotty that she'd be okay. I went to stand, but Jono stopped me.

"No, you're doing a great job. Stay there, keep her calm. Den, get on the four-wheeler and patrol. Radio in if there are other calves being birthed or if you see any threats."

"No worries." The words were barely out of his mouth before he was jogging away towards the bikes we'd been riding. Jono and Scottie worked as a team, barely needing a word between them to help mumma cow birth her calf. She was mooing, grunting, and whining as they pulled the calf's legs free of her body.

"Your calf's coming, Mumma. I know it hurts. I can't imagine how much, but Mabel's nearly here. Scottie's got you. He'll make sure you're okay." I rambled on and on, talking to the cow and stroking her head in my lap. Scottie sat on his arse, his legs propped against the cow's hindquarters and pulled. Heaving the calf out of her. More of the calf's legs appeared, then its rump, and I noticed it was a male, not a female calf. From there, things moved quicker than I'd ever imagined. By the time Jono shifted, ready to help Scottie, the calf's stomach, shoulders and head had appeared. It lay sprawled on top of Scottie as its front legs were freed and Jono quickly rolled it off him so Scottie could get out of the way and wipe off the goopy bloodied mess he was covered in. "He's here, Dotty. Mabel's here. Well done" I stroked her head again but frowned when she went silent in my arms. "Scottie," I called in a panic, shaking the cow's head. "Come on, Mum," I begged. "You've got to be okay. You've got a baby here and he's beautiful. Get up!"

She shook her head, like she was shaking off the pain of the birth and shifted. Scottie was instantly behind me, dragging me backwards. "You did it," he beamed. It was as if he'd won the lotto, sunshine beaming from his smile. "But you've gotta move away from the cows as soon as the calving's over. Dotty's one of our poddy calves. She's tamer than most, but she'll trample you if you're in her way when she's getting up."

I watched, awed from my spot sitting at Scottie's feet on the dirt, as the cow turned to her calf, licking him clean and then waiting for him to suckle. When he did, I couldn't help but cry happy tears. The happiest. Seeing new life brought into this world was uplifting. Raw and kinda disgusting, but amazing too. Scottie crouched down next to me. "You okay?" He smiled and I laughed, nodding and wiping my tears away.

"You saved them and now there's a new calf."

"I couldn't have done it without your help. You're a natural." He held out his hand—the cleanish one—as he stood and added, "Need a hand up?" I grinned and let him haul me up, not resisting when he hooked an arm around my shoulders and pulled me close. "You're almost a local now."

"I'm sure I'll still be a tourist in twenty years' time."

"That's about right," Jono chipped in from beside me, playfully slapping me on the back. "Well done, Macca. You did good. Now, why don't the two of you take the ute, get cleaned up and get some rest. Den and I'll start the next shift early."

Scottie nodded. "Yeah, I stink."

Ma had just woken up when we arrived. Standing in the kitchen dressed in a knee-length white nightdress, she was waiting for the kettle to boil to make some tea. The moment she saw Scottie, she closed her eyes, as if she was dreading the news. "How many did we lose?"

"None," he replied cheerily, the excitement in his voice palpable. "Dotty and her calf are both fine for the moment. Pete did a great job keeping her calm. The calf started suckling straight away. He was a good size too."

"Mabel," I added after he'd finished speaking. "The calf's name is Mabel."

"Ah…" Ma furrowed her brow and tilted her head as if she wanted to say something.

"It's okay." I held my hand up in a stopping motion. "I know I probably won't be able to tell the difference between Mabel and any of the others, and Mabel is usually a female's name, but that's what he's called. Okay? Good. Great. Glad we have that sorted." I chuckled at Ma's wide-eyed stare. She was trying not to laugh, but she failed, and it set me off too.

"Mabel," Scottie turned to me and grinned, "was breach. Pete kept Dotty calm during the whole calving. Jono and Den are out there now. We'll go back out again soon."

"Mabel's special then." She smiled, turning off the heat when the kettle started to whistle. "Good job. I'm glad we didn't lose either one of them." She scrunched up her nose and pointed to Scottie, waving him away. "For goodness' sake, go get cleaned up. You stink to high heaven."

Twelve

Scottie

P ete followed me into our bathroom, closing and locking the door behind us. We'd traded head jobs and hand jobs and engaged in plenty of frottage since I'd started feeling better, and I wanted him again. Seeing him in action, staying calm and speaking to my favourite of all the poddy cows, and that we'd had saved both her and Mabel, it had me wanting to climb him like a tree. But when I looked at him, he was stalking forwards. Our eyes locked and I moaned. Reaching out to undo the buttons of my flannie, he pressed himself up against me, never breaking our stare. I shrugged my shirt off, kicking it into the corner. My jeans went next, his fingers fumbling the metal button and fly, before he pushed the denim over my hips and dragged them down my legs. Pete fell to a crouch before me and looked up at me. I licked my lips, loving him in that position, and Pete tugged off my jeans, finding the tops of my socks and yanking them off too. He ran his nose up my leg, and that tiny touch had my world tilting. I braced myself against the vanity. His eyes drifted closed as he nuzzled his face against my package, and I sucked in a breath. He hummed and looked back up at me, tonguing my hardening shaft through my cotton undies. My head fell back, and I shuddered, my cock hardening as he blew out a hot breath over me. He skirted his palms up my legs. I loved the feel of them, those big palms and long fingers skirting over my muscles, the crisp hairs on my legs standing on end as goosebumps broke out from his touch. I wanted him to swallow me whole, drink me down. I wanted him around me or inside me.

He curled his fingers over the elastic waistband of my black briefs and tugged them down, freeing my arse first before slowing and letting my hardened cock slap back against my stomach. A shock of sensation travelled through me, and I grunted. My undies were tossed aside and the next moment, my Bonds singlet was sailing to the corner where he'd carelessly flung my clothes. He stood, still fully dressed, while I was naked before him. He took me in, his gaze burning a trail down my body. We were so different. I was all angles and golden skin and he was pale and slim. Young. Perfect. The dusting of greying hair on my chest used to make me self-conscious. I'd lamented that I wouldn't be able to pick up in clubs for much longer, my body aging. And yet the way Pete looked at me, made me feel like a damn supermodel. Freaking Chris Hemsworth. Or maybe more of a Hugh Jackman, given our ages. His eyes, green as emeralds, were shining. Desire sparked in their depths. His pupils were blown, his chest heaving as he sucked in ragged breath after ragged breath. Pete's lips, pink and moist from him licking them, had me wanting to lean in and devour him. He was hungry, and I was starving.

He fingered the hair on my chest, the few greys multiplying more recently. My abs had disappeared, but I hadn't gained weight. If anything, I'd lost some from being so sick. My recovery over the last few months meant that I hadn't been as active, but he didn't seem to mind. He eye-fucked me, the bulge in his faded jeans telling me he liked what he saw.

He bit down on his lip and sucked in a breath, his chest expanding before his nose crinkled, and his lips pursed. "The smell of cows and calving is not something I want to be breathing in right now. Let's start with a shower."

I barked out a laugh as he grabbed the bucket and filled it with hot water, Pete directing me to stand in the shower while he got ready. He stripped out of his clothes with no finesse, tossing them aside to join my own as we waited for the bucket to fill. The one thing in Brisbane that I loved—in fact, the only thing I missed when I came back from the city—was the water. The ability to fill a bathtub deep enough to sit in and soak. We'd gone for an early morning swim in the heated pool overlooking the sprawling Brisbane River while the palm trees swayed in the humid breeze. Here it was so dry. Every drop was precious. Sacred. There was no spare water. There wouldn't ever be any long showers for Pete and me, steaming the room and screwing around until the water ran cold. It'd waste half our stores, and we always need to conserve every drop. He turned off the tap and carried the bucket into the shower, his cock bobbing with each step he took. I groaned, sucking my bottom lip into my mouth and biting down. Fuck, I wanted him. He shuddered like he needed to be on the receiving end of my mouth.

Our wash was a haze of hands and lips, soapy sponges and bodies sliding against each other, slippery and sudsy. Pinning me against the wall, he touched every inch of my body he could reach. And I reciprocated. He moaned into my shoulder as I slipped one then two fingers into him, and he gripped our cocks tight, and I fucked into his fist. He bit me, sucking on the skin of my throat as he bucked, on the brink of his orgasm. "I need to be inside you," I grated out, pulling my fingers free and pushing his hips back. He cried out, yanked back from the edge of ecstasy.

"Fuck," he panted. "Fuck." He banged his head against my chest.

"Shh," I soothed. "I'll make it worth your while. You'll wanna scream so loud the whole station will hear you."

"Nngrf," he groaned, slapping his hand against the wall as he shuddered. My cock was hard enough to hammer nails, and I could just picture his hole clenching as he fought back the desire ricocheting through him enough that he could think.

I needed in him. For us to be connected like my body demanded. Without thinking, I dumped half the bucket over me and the rest over him, before I wrapped him in a towel and led him out to the bedroom. At the bed, I nudged him on and hummed as he crawled up it. Pete presented his arse to me, reminding me of that power bottoming energy he emitted during the grand relocate the wombat plan. He was temptation personified. "Stay like that. Exactly like that," I rasped, my voice sounding as if I had swallowed nails. I paused, admiring the view of his long, lean limbs, pale skin, and small pink hole, clenching tight. "Hug the pillow."

He grasped the downy cushion and dragged it across the soft sheets, burying his face in it. I couldn't keep my hands off him, need overwhelming me. I spread his cheeks and leaned in close, blowing a hot breath over his star. He shivered and whimpered, the sounds muffled. "That's it, babe. Feel me." I scraped my teeth over my cheek, biting down and licking away the sting as I moved my hands, my callused skin gliding down his hairy arse to his legs, and back up. I wanted to ride him, to push into him and feel him swallowing me. I ran my hands over his sides to his shoulders and pulled him back against me, mimicking the action. My iron-hard cock was wedged between his perfectly rounded globes, and he pushed back, shuddering at our connection. I ground down against him, need overwhelming me. Desperation clawed at me, my focus singular: get inside him, make him come. Make myself come. He reached out blindly, patting the sheets. He was too far from the bedside table drawers where we kept the rubbers and lube.

"More," he moaned. "I need you."

I didn't fuck around.

Need ignited my actions, lighting a fire underneath me to get moving. I shifted, reaching for our supplies and pressed against him again before tearing the foil wrapper, and unceremoniously rolling on the condom. I squeezed the lube onto it. The wet slick dripped down my covered shaft down his crack. I was burning up, desire searing through me. I couldn't wait. I coated myself, using more lube than I'd ever used before, and rubbed the clear liquid around his hole. I'd had my fingers in him earlier. I just hoped I didn't hurt him now. I gentled, pressing forward slowly. Just enough to stretch his hole around my girth. He tried pushing back, driving himself onto me, but I held Pete steady. It took everything in me to stop him. To not rock forward and plunge deep inside. The corded muscle along Pete's back strained, and the frustrated mewling muffled by the pillow had me grinding my teeth together, using willpower alone to hold back. I massaged his hole as it stretched around my cockhead, a heated wonder filling my gaze as I watched myself slowly disappear inside him. His pucker loosened, and I inched forward, slowly pressing deeper. He moaned softly, and I tightened my fingers around his hips. "Fuck," I moaned. "You feel so good."

He choked out a moan and stretched his arms out in front of him, arching his back and clenching tight, shuddering at my touch. I hissed as he swallowed me deeper and the thread of control I'd held onto snapped. I ran my hands up his back, loving the bend in his spine as he lifted his arse higher. Gripping his shoulders, I surged forward. He cried out and I ground my hips down, pressing hard against his arse. Pressure built with every thrust of my hips. Short, sharp jabs and longer rolls. I kept moving, changing up my rhythm until he was scrambling, trying to grip onto the sheets below his hands. My orgasm was like waves lapping at the top of a levee, about to breach and slide over me. But I needed more.

I pulled out and Pete scrambled, making a noise somewhere between a sob and a shout into the pillow he had muffling the animalistic noises he was making. Cold air rushed around my cock and my orgasm ebbed. "I need to see you," I apologized, falling gracelessly onto the bed next to him. He turned his face to me, and my breath caught. His eyes were the most intense green I'd ever seen, with fire in their depths. "Ride me, babe," I pleaded. He didn't hesitate, gripping my hand and linking our fingers together before he clambered on top of me. I stroked up and down my iron-hard shaft, holding it steady as he slid down and rocked, riding me slowly. I savoured the feel of being inside him. All wet heat and silken smoothness, as if we were made for each other. He gasped as I planted my feet and thrust upwards, my hips meeting Pete's while I plunged deep inside him. Thrust for thrust, we moved together, gasping breaths, moans, and grunts as he rode me. The waters rose, lapping at the tops of the embankment again. I was dipping a toe in, getting ready to be washed away by the orgasm that would crash over me at any moment. I pushed up to almost sitting, my arms stretched out behind me to help hold me up. Pete wrapped himself around me, his hands in my hair, and his knees bracketing my hips. Slamming his mouth against mine, he kissed me. A fission of electricity travelled down my spine at our touch. Our kisses were hungry, frantic as I fed him my moans, and he gifted me with his. Chest to chest, he rode me, his cock trapped between our stomachs.

I wrapped an arm around his waist and pulled him closer, my hips stuttering as I moaned long and low. I tipped my head back, sucking in a breath, and Pete moved his mouth to my throat, sucking and licking on my skin. It was as if he was as desperate to taste me, as I was him. "I'm close," I groaned. "Touch yourself."

He didn't need to. He rocked his hips again, and the gasp left me in no doubt that I'd hit his prostate dead on. He breathed deep, burying his face into the crook of my neck as I rocked again, keeping him pressed against me. The ripple of his channel around me made the buzz at the base of my spine notch up a level and radiate outwards in rippling waves. He gripped my hair and pulled my mouth to his again, before moaning loudly as his orgasm hit. I swallowed his sounds as stripes of his cum painted my stomach, and I choked out a cry against his lips, bucking into him. The force of my orgasm, weeks in the making, made me collapse back. I pulled him with me, and we sucked in heaving breaths as I rode out the tingling in my limbs and the buzz from the high. Lazy kisses against my cheek and temple had me shifting so I could capture his lips, and we kissed slowly, our tongues meeting and caressing.

He winced as I pulled out, and I cursed myself at my impatience. I shifted my fingers, running them around his rim. "Did I hurt you?" I whispered, wishing I'd taken more time to prep him. He shook his head and I finally breathed, then moaned as he rocked his hips, rubbing his half-hard shaft against my own sensitive one. "You want more?" I rasped, internally cheering like I'd scored a try at a State of Origin decider when he nodded. I rolled and slid off the condom, tossing it to the side of the bed as I kissed my way down his stomach. Licking up his salty cum, I hummed and pressed my lips to every place I could reach. Down to his knees, and up the sensitive inside of his legs to his hips and up to his armpits, breathing in his scent. I showered him in soft sucks and licks and playful bites, never letting up the massage on the sensitive spots on his hips. I kept going until he was hard and wanting, need making his breaths ragged. Then I ran my hand over my own shaft until I was engorged and hard. "You ready?" I asked after he practically melted into the mattress when I nibbled at his hip, my tongue snaking out to follow the line of muscle that led to his cock like a stair-way to heaven. I sucked him down, pulling his shaft into my throat and he moaned, struggling not to thrust into my mouth. I wanted him to lose it, to obliterate his ability to think. I primed him with two fingers, slowly and softly feel-ing inside him until I found the spongy pad of his prostate. When he was a writhing, incoherent mess of desire and need, I rolled on another condom and slid inside him. Nir-vana. Heat and clenching muscle gripped me, the slick from the lube giving me a frictionless slide so I could light him up. I rolled my hips slowly and made love to him until he shot us clear over those levees, straight to the stars.

He was already asleep when I'd wiped him down and slipped the soft covering over him. When I slid in behind him, he mumbled something to me, and I whispered into his hair that I loved him, wishing I had the courage to tell him when he was conscious. I didn't know why I couldn't.

Maybe it was something to do with my dad, maybe I still wasn't sure he'd stay, but I forced down the fear. I was determined to enjoy whatever time we had together without regret. If that meant cocooning him in my arms, so he was wrapped up and protected by the love I couldn't yet express, then I would.

Pete hadn't been into the guest house in weeks, spending every night in my bed. We'd slip out early to do the morning chores that had, over time, become ours rather than mine alone. On the days that we did the night shift, we'd wait until the house was quiet and slip into my bedroom. But as much as I loved having him in my bed, I had to send him away. As much as it killed me, I needed to tell him to go.

Spring was warming up fast, already in the mid-thirties every day. At nearly ninety-five on the old scale, the dry and blustery weather would only get worse as summer neared. Pete couldn't wait any longer to go out prospecting before his window would close for at least the next four months, right up until midway through autumn. It was just too hot out here. Too dangerous. And there was no way I was risking him so that he could prove a legend.

He was still fast asleep, lying with his head on my chest and leg across mine, his arm wrapped around my waist. He'd crawled into my arms after a horror night of calving.

We'd lost two calves during our loop around the herd. Wild dogs had stolen in and attacked, leaving a trail of blood and spooked cows behind them. There were paw prints every-where, the pack of hunters large. I'd suspected dingoes at first, but after seeing the paw prints, I knew they weren't the culprits. Feral dogs and crossbreeds had larger litters and were often bigger. More numerous than dingoes, they were also far more dangerous.

Pete was wrecked by the loss of the two calves. Tears had streamed down his cheeks, but he'd stoically taken a deep breath, wiped his eyes, and moved on. When we'd found the cow in trouble, and I hadn't been able to save her, he'd withdrawn inside himself, his face going a ghostly white and the spark fading from his eyes. He was over-whelmed, and absolutely gutted by the deaths we'd expe-rienced that night. Powerlessness had stolen over me, ripping me raw. It was nature, something I'd grown up with. I'd experienced the loss that goes with raising cattle in the outback for decades. It still hurt, but it was muted too, the knowledge that it was nature at work was as much comfort as the cause of the feeling of injustice. Seeing Pete go through it for the first time, broke my heart.

I'd radioed Ally, and she and the boys had taken over while I led him inside, bathed him, and held him tight for the rest of the night. Now, the sun was blazing overhead, the ceiling fan above our bed spinning in fast circles, but not cooling the thick air enough to make it comfortable. The corner of the sheet covered one of my legs and Pete's arse as he lay diagonally on the bed, using my chest as a pillow.

Now it was time for us to wake and for Pete to get on with his plan. He'd come here months earlier with a mission, and fate had intervened, throwing one distraction after another in front of him. He'd never protested once, jumping into station life and experiencing everything on offer. When I'd fallen sick, he'd taken over all my more menial, but physically demanding tasks, completing them without ever protesting. He'd woken up at the arse crack of dawn, as he liked to call the pre-sunrise twilight, and without the aid of coffee, had fed the animals and shovelled shit. Then calving season had arrived, and for another few weeks, we'd worked six-hour rotating shifts, our sleep patterns off, and mealtimes scattered around, leaving us to eat whenever we could. We patrolled the herd, loaded up any poddy calves, and brought them back to the springer paddock for hand-rearing. We'd done patch jobs on fences which had come down, and everything else except the one thing he was here for.

He snuggled closer, his arm tightening around my waist. I pressed a kiss to his hair and ran my fingertips over his spine, wishing I could reach more of him to press kisses to. He hummed sleepily, and I played dirty, running my hand up his leg and rubbing the spot just inside his hip bone. He moaned and rocked forward, rubbing his filling cock against my leg. "Greedy today," I murmured.

"Mmm," he murmured sleepily. "Always." He ran his hand up my chest and lifted his head to meet mine, kissing me slowly. It was all tongues tangling and lips sliding against each other's, and I held him tighter as we made out. Pulling back reluctantly, I nudged my nose against his. When he leaned in to kiss me again, I shifted back, needing to speak with him before we got carried away. "What is it?" he asked, propping himself up on one elbow to look at me properly. Long red lashes framed green eyes, eyes that I could get lost in. They were dark with worry, sharp and focussed on me as his brow furrowed.

"You need to go," I started, pausing as his face fell, then continued on in a rush when I realized what I hadn't said. "Prospecting. I want you to go prospecting. It's getting warmer every day. There isn't much time before it'll be too hot to be out at the ravine at all. As it is, you're only going to be able to do a few hours at a time, and not during the middle of the day. If you wait too much longer, it'll be too dangerous to be out there at all." I leaned in and kissed him. "I can't risk you, Pete. You've been invaluable here, but now is your last chance to do your thing before summer. To confirm that you were right about Byron."

He nodded slowly, but he laid his head back on my shoulder, curling into me. Maybe curling in on himself. "What happens if it's not there? What happens if I go out there, and there's no reading again? If I've wasted years looking for something that just doesn't exist?" He looked up at me, his eyes shining with emotion. With pleading and desperation.

"If you don't go out, you'll never know." I leaned in and kissed him softly, my lips lingering against his.

"But I can't be disappointed then," he whispered. "It'll stay a mystery." He shrugged against my shoulder, acting as if he didn't care, but I knew how much it meant to him. How much he'd invested in getting this far.

"Byron's gold is here. I know it." I pushed back a lock of his hair from his freckled forehead and gazed into his eyes. Trailing my fingertips down his face, along his throat to the dip at his clavicle, I leaned in again and kissed him. Slower this time. A press of lips together, whisper soft. "You're going to find his outback treasure."

"You can't come, can you?" he asked,

"No. I can't, not with calving." Disappointment shined in his eyes, and I was sure it was reflected in mine too. I wanted to go, but I had a responsibility to the cows and their calves. We needed someone with the training to help the cows if they needed it, and it wasn't fair to leave Jono and Ally to cover me.

We plotted and planned his trip. I didn't want him to go alone like he was offering. I hated the idea of him out there by himself, but he wouldn't hear of taking another stockman away from the station when we needed everyone on board. We did, but it didn't matter; he still wasn't going alone. We had a bull who'd wandered off from the rest of the mob, his tracking device showing him a good twenty Ks away from the others. There'd be a bit of a drive to get to him through the paddocks, but it was doable. So I suggested Waru go with him, and while Pete was prospecting, he could check on the bull. If they left after lunch the next day, they could spend two nights there and the equivalent of two full days prospecting. It'd be enough for Pete to get a read on whether there was any truth to his suspicion that there was gold in the ravine. If there was, then we could figure out how to best recover it without destroying the landscape, implementing our plan as soon as the weather cooled down enough in autumn.

All he had to do was load a tin of coffee that he'd nearly forgotten from his supplies—the whole trip would have been a disaster without it. I'd counted everything out—water, enough food for two people for the two days, and the basic kitchen supplies they needed to reheat it, a full tank of fuel, two sat phones and a charging cable, swags and fire starters, the shotgun, and Pete's prospecting equipment. Now I was standing at the driver door of his ute, my hands on the doorframe, while Pete buckled up his seat belt. Waru was already sitting next to him, and it gave me comfort knowing that someone as experienced in the outback as Waru would be with him most of the time—it was the only reason why I wasn't having a nervous breakdown over the idea of him going out there.

"Remember, any problems with the ute, stay with it. If Waru is late, whatever you do, don't go looking for him. Stay at the gully with the water and call me. I'll come and get you." I stared at him until he nodded. Waru was taking the ute to find the bull. He'd leave the big water tank with Pete and take the smaller one with him. It was one of the most important things I needed Pete to remember. He'd die if he left the safety of his water supply. "Call me if you need anything and I'll come straight out. Drink as much as you need if you're thirsty, then have some more. Don't ration the water or you'll get dehydrated, but measure what you're having so you know you're drinking enough. There should be more than you'll need, but if you start to run low, come back." I didn't give him a chance do any more than nod, my words coming out in a rush. "The sat phone is charged and the home number's programmed in. Call if you need us. I don't care what time it is, just call. Check in when you get there so I know you're both safe. Don't put your hands between any rocks or try to shift any. Snakes generally won't strike unless they're threatened by you, so if you see any, just back away slowly." Pete rolled his eyes at me, but I saw him stiffen at the mention of snakes. "If you do get bitten, use the compression bandage. Demobilise your entire limb. Once you've done that, call me. I'll get the chopper out there and get you straight into Longreach, okay?"

This time he didn't nod. He grasped my forearm and squeezed, his eyes smiling warmly. "We'll be okay. I'll have Waru with me for most of the time we're out there. I've learnt a lot camping with you. I won't take any stupid risks."

I closed my eyes and nodded, my heart screaming at me not to let him go, but he was a grown man, and he'd worked far too hard on this for me to stand in his way. He needed to know that even if I couldn't be with him, I'd support him all the way. "Be safe and come home."

"We will." He squeezed my forearm once more and let go, turning the engine over and putting the ute in gear.

"See you in a couple of days." I smiled at him and rapped on the doorframe, a quick double tap. "Good luck."

He smiled at me, and I watched as he drove away, my heart going with him. It seemed like a lifetime ago—and yet only a heartbeat of time out here in the outback—that Pete had arrived. Looking back at what he was like when he arrived, he'd been full of hope and confidence that, in some respects, had been misplaced. He was better prepared now, having cut his teeth in the desert with Ally, me, and our hands by his side. Now he had every chance of finding Byron's gold and surviving to tell the tale. All I had to do was sit and wait for him to call in and eventually return. It was going to be easier said than done.

THIRTEEN

Pete

Waru was setting up camp in the same spot that Scottie and I had chosen when we'd been here a few months earlier. He hadn't commented about our exchange when we'd left, but Scottie had made it obvious that he cared more than as a mate. I didn't know what he'd say about it, whether he'd care, or if being gay in Aboriginal culture was as unacceptable as in some others. I supposed I'd find out sooner or later.

I had my headphones on and was listening for the whine of the detector. Searching for any trace of metal. Gold in particular. The first dip and buzz of the detector sounded about an hour in. First a nail. Then a tin mug, like the ones used by travellers last century. Then more evidence of a camp—a fork, a rusted tin, and finally a trowel. The odds were long, but I'd bet on longer odds before. My degrees and the mass of research I'd accumulated on Byron and his fabled gold-laden quartz reef were a testament to that. With every hum of the metal detector, my excitement spiked. Could this be it? Could it be the beginning of my find? I kept going, long into the afternoon, and then I heard it. The tone being emitted changed. A strong signal. One that was dense. As strong a tone as I'd heard when I'd found the trowel, the mug, and the can. But was it more of the same? Evidence of an expedition leaving a footprint decades after they'd traversed these red lands? I used my plastic trowel to dig a shallow hole in the sandy loam, running the detector over the disturbed surface. Whatever was setting the sensor off was still buried. I dug further, finding quartz rocks disbursed with the red dirt. Then I saw it.

Gold.

Muted red from being buried, but it was undoubtedly gold. A tiny nugget of it. I ran the trowel over the detector, and it pinged. I'd found gold.

My heart slammed against my chest. My breath coming in quick bursts. I wanted to jump out of my skin. Dance in the rain and sing while spinning from lampposts. I choked out a cheer and cleaned off the piece, barely double the size of a peppercorn, holding it in the fading light to get a better look at it. It was gold! Waru was standing a couple of hundred metres away at the camp, but he wasn't the person I wanted to tell. I pulled my sat phone out of my pocket and dialled Scottie's home number. Ma picked it up. "Hello?"

"Hi, Ma. It's me. It's Pete. Is Scottie there?" I rushed out.

"Sure, hon. Is everything okay? You all right?"

"Yes, yeah. Absolutely. I just need to speak to Scottie urgently."

"Okay," she hedged, calling out for him. Footsteps sounded, Scottie running to the phone.

"Pete, you okay?"

"I found it, Scottie. I found gold," I cried, my excitement spilling over.

A pause, then he spoke, his excitement palpable. "You found it?"

"I did." I laughed. "I bloody did. It's tiny. Like a quarter of my fingernail, but it's… it's gold. It's here."

"I'm so proud of you, babe. So, so proud. Well done." His voice was choked with emotion, all the longing and love that was erupting in me, reflected in both the words he spoke and Scottie's tone. "You're gonna keep going, right? Keep detecting tomorrow?"

"Yeah, I am. And even if it's not Byron's reef, it's ours now."

We said our goodbyes, and I marked the spot, tapping a stake into the ground where I'd detected to. I didn't have much light left, and if I kept going, I wouldn't be able to make my way back to Waru and the camp without a torch. And seeing the fallout of the wild dog attack on our calves had left me spooked. There was no way I was going to be alone out here at any time of night.

I jogged back to the camp and held out the nugget to Waru, grinning like a fool. "Nice work," he praised. "Is it the reef?"

"I don't know. Honestly, I don't care anymore. I've found gold. All that work, all the studying. The debt." I huffed. My university debt was so high that I was too scared to check the balance. "It's all been worth it. I followed the environment, identified the markers, found gold."

"And Scottie?" His words were quiet. Measured. But they had an undeniable force behind them. Waru was a man trying to protect his friend. But our relationship wasn't just my secret to tell. Admitting anything to him would out Scottie. I hated lying to his face, but I didn't have a choice. I wouldn't hurt Scottie by talking about our relationship behind his back. I bit down on my lip, despising myself for the untruth I was about to tell.

"His friendship means everything to me."

Waru glared at me, his jaw tight and his nostrils flaring. "Yeah. Good," he huffed. His disbelief was palpable.

The rest of the night passed by uncomfortably. Waru barely spoke, answering my questions with one-worded replies. Finally, I'd had enough. "Waru, look, I know what I said before pissed you off, but it's none of your damn business what the details of Scottie and my friendship is. We're mates." I inwardly cringed at the comment and had to force myself to continue uninterrupted. "We're close. He's important to me. I'm not using him. You have to believe that."

"He considers you family. He cares for you, protects you. He's a good man." He left unsaid his next statement, but the warning hung clear in the air—don't fuck this up. Don't use or abuse him. Or I'd have Waru and undoubtedly every other person at Pearce Station to contend with.

"He is. The best." I met his gaze and didn't waver. After a moment, Waru's lips quirked up in the tiniest of smiles, and he nodded.

"Glad you understand." He laid down then, sliding into his swag on the opposite side of the fire to me. "Night, Pete."

"Night, Waru." I rolled onto my back, gazing up at the sky. The blanket of stars overhead looked so close that I could touch them. The moonless night was darker than usual, but the stars were spectacular, lighting up the sky with a wondrous brilliance. Billions of tiny pinpricks of light. Uninterrupted across the sky from horizon to horizon. I wished Scottie was there with me. The night would have been perfect with him there, but I understood why he needed to be at the homestead. Truth be told, I was surprised he could get away the last time he'd come. I weighed the tiny nugget in my hand, heavy for an object of its size, and smiled into the night. I slipped it into my duffel bag, the same one I always used as a pillow, and closed my eyes. For the first time since hearing of Byron's tall tale, I knew why gold mesmerized people.

I got started early, the sun barely up before I was stoking the fire and bringing a billy of water to the boil. Waru and I had our mugs at the ready, me with instant coffee and him with a Bushells tea bag. We ate a breakfast of vegemite toast and a couple of protein balls and packed up our things before Waru stomped out the fire making sure it was completely out. We unloaded the larger of the water tanks and propped it in the shade among a copse of trees together with food for me for the day, then packed both the swags into the ute. Keeping them there would stop creepy crawlies making a home in them during the heat of the day, or worse, a snake.

"You got your sat phone?" I asked Waru.

"Yep, and you've got yours." He pointed to the yellow smartphone in my hand. We went through our plans for the day, the check-in times, and the times he wanted me resting in the shade. I double-checked I had a hat, sunscreen, and sunnies, my prospecting equipment, and a small canister to store any gold I found. We broke apart, and I found my spot and kept searching. It wasn't long until I got another hit, and after that, they kept on coming. Small nuggets, ranging from tiny like the one I'd picked up the day before to a few the size of small marbles. Each one was within the topsoil, but there was no way Byron could have discovered the gold simply by stumbling on the reef perchance. It just wasn't visible. Maybe he read the markers like me, maybe he turned over a rock and found a nugget sitting there at surface level, and his tale grew taller with every retelling of it until the singular nugget was a whole reef of gold and pristine white quartz.

My thoughts were interrupted when my detector whined, a louder longer signal than I'd heard before. It was close. And whatever it was, was big. I dug down, turning over soil and ran the detector over it again. Still in the ground. I dug further, creating a larger hole. A handspan deep and the detector squealed through the headphones, making me wince. I pushed the trowel in and hit something hard. A rock, quartz, another can, who knew. But I kept going and managed to dig around the object, confirming that it was a rock—a piece of quartz the size of a baseball. It didn't explain why the detector screamed in my ears though. I brushed off the red dirt clumped to the crystal and fell back onto my arse. "What the hell?" I mumbled, seeing the vein of colour through the middle of the reddish-brown rock. I tipped a few drops of water onto it and my eyes widened. A seam of gold ran through the quartz. It was a beautiful sample of decorative gold, by far the largest I'd found so far.

I stood up and stretched my back, trying to roll the kinks out of my tired muscles. I pulled off my headphones and tilted my neck from side to side, enjoying being out in the open. I listened, expecting to hear the noises of the outback—the piercing cry of an eagle, the hum of cicadas, but there was nothing. It was quiet, the silence almost suffocating. A little eerie too. The only thing I could hear came from the quiet rustle of the eucalypt branches. But maybe it was just because of where I was, deep in the ravine. The quartz and red dirt reached up high around me, the walls seemingly closing in. Dried grass and brittle desert shrubs surrounded me, a large eucalypt towering above. The sky, streaked with dirty looking clouds, wasn't its normal brilliant blue, but it didn't lessen the intensity of the sun. It still beat down on me relentlessly. Even in the heat, though, the reef was beautiful. Like everything else in this landscape, it was a study in extremes. White quartz sparkled as if it were diamond-encrusted, interspersed among patches of vibrant red dirt and blue-grey scrubby bushes.

I should have already stopped for a break. Sweat slid down my back, between my shoulder blades and I lifted my wide-brimmed hat, wiping my brow with the back of my gloved hand. The metal detector was starting to get heavy, my arms aching from holding it. I took a swig of my half-empty drink bottle and rolled my shoulders again, trying to relax the muscles I didn't even realize had tensed up. The weight in my pocket was significant. It made me smile, not because I was striking it rich, but because I felt vindicated. Like it hadn't been a waste of my time pursuing my degrees, that my investment of endless hours studying and research-ing was worth it in some small way. I'd found gold. Regard-less of whether it was Byron's gold, it was still gold. If my guess on how much it weighed was correct, I was holding a good twenty grand in my pocket. It had taken me a while to get there—years in fact—but staying was my only priority. In the grand scheme, I didn't care if I found one more gram of gold. Having Scottie and his family waiting for me, wel-coming me home was the only reward I needed. But being able to contribute to the station in a meaningful way would be nice. Had I solved the question of whether Byron's reef existed? I didn't know, but I didn't really care either way an-ymore. Scottie was my reason for staying. This land, this sta-tion, had drawn me in. It'd been calling me for years. A circuitous route had finally led me here, but now that I'd made it, I'd realized I was home. Gold or no gold, Scottie was my home.

I pulled out a handful of nuts and dried fruit—macada-mias, mango, and banana—and ate as I took a breather. Climbing a little higher on the side of the reef, I lifted myself up on a quartz boulder that reached nearly half my height. Taking another swig of my drink bottle, I downed the contents and finished off my snack. I knew probably shouldn't go any further without water, but another half hour wouldn't hurt anyone. It was warm but no worse than a summer's day in Sydney, and I went hours without water there. Resting my sore legs for a moment, I tilted my head up to the sky and breathed deep, inhaling the dry desert air into my lungs.

I went back to detecting, only going as far as the next tree before deciding to take a break for the hottest part of the day. I'd need water by then, and I had a decent walk back to the tank we'd pulled off the ute. I didn't want to risk getting heatstroke or too dehydrated.

Scottie

I looked up and saw the sky streaked with the grey-brown smoke of a grass fire in the distance. We didn't get many out here. Especially not recently—there wasn't much fuel left to burn—but the grass that remained was bone dry. Fast to ignite, it burnt hot and spread quickly.

The wind was up that day, blowing a gale, but it seemed to be travelling parallel to our station, not towards us. A small shift in the wind though, and it could be a very different story. My heart thudded in my chest and my gut clenched. I wasn't scared of many things, but fire was one of them. And Pete was out there. Nausea swept over me at the thought of him getting stuck out at the ravine. Of him being injured or losing him. Every worst-case scenario flashed in my mind's eye, and panic crawled over me, stealing my breath. I needed him safe. Was I being ridiculous if I asked him to come back? Unreasonable? Overprotective? Hell, I was probably all those things. Logically, I knew Pete could look after himself. He wasn't stupid or irresponsible, but he was also inexperienced in the outback, and I cared too much about him to risk his safety. I didn't want to be an arsehole either. "Ally," I called out to her. Standing near so only she could hear my words, I asked, "Should I call Pete and ask him to come back?" I pointed to the fire. "It's nowhere near us, but that's big enough to have me worried."

"Are you asking me what I'd do if I were dating a city boy, and he was out there, and I was here and there was a fire close by enough to smell smoke?"

"Yeah." I nodded and looked down at her. I was sure she could see how uncertain I was, how torn I was by wanting to wrap him up and keep him safe but knowing that he needed to live his own life too. Pete's entire adult life had been dedicated to discovering the truth about Byron's gold. How could I pull him back when he'd just found an indication that he might be on the right track? He was on the cusp of knowing, of proving his theory. But this fire had me scared.

She smiled softly and clapped me on the shoulder. "I think you already have your answer. But don't forget that Waru's with him. He's not exactly alone out there."

"He *is* alone." I blew out a breath, hating my suggestion that Waru leave him to go check on the damn bull. It was a stupid idea, one that would haunt me until the end of my days if anything happened to Pete. "Waru has the truck. He's checking on the bull. He should be on his way back, but Pete's been alone for most of the morning."

Her eyes widened a fraction before she schooled her features. "I'll go call them. Make sure Waru's on his way back. Get them to come home rather than hanging out there for the afternoon." She squeezed my forearm, and I thanked her quietly before she jogged inside.

I went back to fixing the poddy feeder, trying to distract myself. It wasn't working. I banged around, pulling it apart and putting it back together, but there was still a problem. The milk still wasn't feeding through properly. I huffed, frustration making me grind my teeth together and slam the screwdriver down. "Bugger it," I swore. "Bloody useless piece of shit."

"Want me to give it a go?" Den asked.

"Go for it." I passed him the hand tool and went to walk away.

"Could you hold this for me, Scottie? I think I see what the problem is."

I groaned. "You were waiting for me to see it too, weren't you?" My question wasn't really one. There was no way Den had just discovered the problem, and he didn't bother answering me. Instead, he smiled as he dipped his head, letting me stew in my frustration.

He had the U-shaped bracing unscrewed and pulled part of the clear plastic piping away. I could see the tiny slit in it, just big enough that when the calf sucked, it was getting air, not milk. I held the backing board steady as Den replaced the pipe and re-screwed it all in place. Once finished, we mounted the feeder again. Sitting there, surrounded by the calves wanting to be fed, usually made me smile. I loved seeing those little guys grow, even though their chances of survival were always slimmer than a calf fed by its mother. But today, I couldn't even muster up a single iota of interest in them. Instead, fear rattled around my brain, stunting my ability to think properly.

"Pete and Waru on your mind?" he asked casually, kicking away a rock. "I don't like the look of that fire either."

"Yeah," I muttered. "I'll feel better when both of them are back."

"Why don't I go see if Ally got onto them?" he offered. "No point you worrying about 'em if they're on the way back."

"Could you?" As much as I wanted to march in there and get him home, I didn't. It wouldn't take Pete long to realize that it was me asking him to come back, but hopefully by then, he'd already be on his way. I hated the idea that I was smothering him. But I couldn't let go of the niggling worry in the back of my mind. The flashing caution signs in my brain. Worry had slithered its way down my spine and ratcheted up my blood pressure. Den unhurriedly strolled away, and I huffed out a breath, shaking off the ridiculous feeling. I was overreacting. I had to be. No one else was scared. *But no one else has the love of their life out in the desert alone either.*

It felt like forever before he ducked his head back around the wall of the shed I was working alongside. I'd put a batch of milk into the feeder and got six of the calves started, watching them to make sure they fed properly. "Mate," he started hesitantly, his tone making me freeze in my tracks. "Ally hasn't had any luck. She's trying, but neither of them are picking up." I looked over to him, and concern marred his features. His brows were pinched, his lips a straight line.

"Oh," I breathed. It was all I was capable of. My mind had whited out, filled with static, and my gut screamed that something was wrong. Pete should've had his sat phone with him, and Waru wouldn't be too far away from his either.

"That's not all." He pointed in the general direction of the fire. "I think the wind's shifted."

I walked out from behind the wall, every step like wading through molasses. Grass fires could move at twenty-five clicks, faster if the wind was strong. Embers could jump the fire front, leapfrogging it forwards. If the wind had changed and it was heading towards us, we didn't have much time to get the cattle and horses to safety. If it was heading towards the ravine, we'd have even less.

I looked up and my breath stalled in my lungs. "Fuck," I whispered. Smoke was no longer floating up in the air but being pushed by the winds. And there was no doubt it'd shifted.

The land was burning.

And it was headed straight for Pete.

Terror rushed through me, my blood freezing in my veins. My heart skidded to a stop and I could do nothing except stare in horror as the smoke billowed in the wind, pointing in the direction of the oncoming front. It was as if I'd drawn a line on a map, plotting a course straight for the gully. Straight for Pete. His face flashed before my eyes, his name a tortured whisper on my lips. "Fuck."

Something unlocked in me, my legs moving before I could even think twice. I was sprinting towards the big shed. Skidding in the dirt, I threw myself into the Landcruiser, the door slamming shut as I flipped the sun visor. The key fell and I fumbled it, nearly dropping it before I could get the ignition turned over. Slamming it in gear, I floored it, fishtailing out of the shed. I almost ploughed through the gate, stopping at the last moment when common sense made me think twice. If I punctured the tyre, I wouldn't make it to him in time. I wrenched open the gate and heard Ally screaming, "Scottie," at me. I turned, and she was sprinting to me, her arms full of the heavy woollen blankets we had on our beds during winter. Pure wool, they were the best fire-retardant materials we had. She threw them in the front seat after skidding to a halt. "Get him home. Go."

I was racing a monster. One that was consuming everything in its path. Fire was the great equalizer, completely impersonal in its destructive force. I had to win. There was no other option, because I had everything to lose. The one person who was my everything was out there, up against Mother Nature in all her ferocious glory.

I pressed my foot harder on the accelerator, sending the heavy vehicle careening over bumps and mounds, tearing through bushes and over grasslands. I swerved around trees and dodged boulders, got air coming out of ditches. For every moment I looked forward, I glanced sideways too, checking my progress against the fire. It was racing me, picking up speed as I drove frantically towards the man I'd give everything for. I hadn't told him I loved him. I tried to show him with every touch, in every moment between us. Why hadn't I been brave enough? Why hadn't I tossed caution to the wind and shouted it from the top of the damn shed? Why hadn't I told him the countless times we'd been together? Why hadn't I announced it right there in the pub when I'd gone grovelling to him in Longreach? Even earlier. On the muster? Standing at the windmill when we'd ridden off together, or in the chopper? When he'd listened in wonder to the dreamtime stories Waru told? When we'd talked over the bonfire on his first night on the station? When he'd seen me with Tilly and we'd locked eyes, connecting after only having known each other for a moment in time? I cursed my stupidity and pushed the four-by-four harder, determined that my last words to Pete wouldn't be "good luck." There was no way our story was ending. I wouldn't let it. I'd stood defiant in the face of adversity before and won. This was no different. This fire would not beat us. It couldn't because the alternative was unfathomable.

The two-hour trip passed by in a heart-stopping forty minutes. I had the pedal to the metal the whole way there. I saw their campsite first, the ring of rocks and the small burnt-out fire. The ravine started up ahead, and the vege-tation—dry grasses and scrubby bushes—grew denser around it the farther into quartz reef a person travelled. It widened up ahead too, yawning open into more of a lake formation. The water, when it flooded, slowed its path there, and the vegetation drank it up, flourishing at its banks. Pete could be anywhere in the kilometres-long stretches of white quartz crystal. I hung a right, turning the car as I spotted the water tank Waru had pulled off the ute. In the shade of a copse of eucalypts, it was Pete's water supply for the day. He had to be close. I prayed to the spirits of this land that he was.

I couldn't drive into the gully. Quartz boulders, some as high as the wheels of the Landcruiser made the path impos-sible to follow. So, I trailed along the edge of the narrow ravine as it snaked its way closer to the fire front, gradually growing deeper as it traversed my land. Smoke billowed in front of me, cutting down my visibility. The fire was getting closer. Now that I was travelling directly at it, it was gaining on us like a tsunami. A great wall of impenetrable flames and smoke. Embers flew at the car, hitting the windscreen as I flew forwards. I took a breath and steeled my nerves, thinking of Pete as I sped up, tearing along the edge of the ten feet deep chasm searching for him.

Then he was there, up ahead. One hand was held over his mouth as he coughed, looking for shelter as he ran blindly between boulders of white quartz, tripping on rocks as he looked over his shoulder. I slammed on the brakes, coming to a lurching halt and hit the horn. His eyes snapped to mine, and I was out of the car in an instant, scrambling over to the edge of the ravine, screaming frantically at him to come to me. It was too deep for Pete to climb out. Too deep for me to reach in and help pull him up too, but I had a winch.

"Pete, hold on, I'm coming," I yelled, the panic in my voice making it wobble. The remote for the winch was in the glove box. I scrambled there, throwing open the compartment and yanking everything out, my movements desperate. Finally, at the bottom, I found it. I didn't have time to breathe a sigh of relief. The radiant heat from the fire had reached us, cooking my skin as it announced the arrival of the front. I had minutes to spare, if that. Unspooling the winch, I tossed down the thick hook to Pete, and he jumped for it, grasping onto it as I stopped it from continuing to wind out. "You got it, babe?"

"Yeah." He nodded, watching the smoke billow as it boiled and rolled over the fire gaining on us. "Scottie, please don't drop me," he begged, his eyes wide with terror. I clenched my jaw tight at the sheer panic in Pete's voice and reversed the winch, starting to wind it in. On my knees on the edge of the ravine, I reached for him, grasping his wrist and hauling him over. Then we were running, rushing to get into the car. I grabbed the detector and tossed it over the back seat, pushing Pete in too.

"Get in the back seat," I ordered, and he scrambled over without question, tossing the detector into the open boot area. I looked around. Dry grass surrounded us, but there was a barren patch behind us. Away from the gully and the trees surrounding its edge along this part of the quartz filled reef. A hundred metres or so. I looked forward and saw nothing but smoke and a red haze. Flames licking the ground. Burning it and consuming the tinder-dry fuel in an instant. The line of fire was upon us. Resolve straightened my spine. Calm settled over me. I needed to do this. I needed to keep Pete safe. Slamming the door closed, I hit reverse and floored it, the tyres spitting dirt and rocks before they grabbed and lurched us towards the clearing. Behind me, Pete whimpered as I over-corrected and he slammed against the door. I shoved the blankets at him. "Wrap up, get on the floor. Drink some water if there's any back there."

Finally, after what felt like an age, we made the clearing. Fire licked at the car, embers pelting the paintwork like rain. I checked the vents, made sure they were closed, turned off the ignition, and scrambled over the back seat, covering Pete's trembling body with my own and dragging the last of the blankets over us. We stayed there like that, the heat overwhelming as the fire raged around. The roar of the burn subsided, and yet I held on. Only when it was quiet, when I could no longer hear the crackle of embers burning, did I risk looking up. There was no visible damage from the inside of the car. The plastic mirrors were still intact, and all the glass had survived. I think the clearing had saved us. I cast my gaze out wider. Blackened grass and shrubs surrounded us. The paddock looked like a wasteland, the lower levels of vegetation disintegrated by the fire. Red dirt stood stark against the blackened skeletal remains of bushes. I breathed a sigh of relief and felt Pete's phone buzz against the seat. Lifting myself off him, and peeling back the blankets, I let him reach for it. Tears tracked lines down his dirty face, and I wiped them away with my thumb, cupping his cheek. I pulled his forehead to mine, kissing him softly as he fisted the front of my shirt and mumbled that he was okay into the phone. I could hear Ally's frantic screeching and I took it off him. "I got to him, Ally. I got him."

"Oh, thank God," she breathed. "We've been trying to call, but he didn't answer."

"What about Waru?"

"He's okay. He should be there any second."

"All right. I'm bringing him home. I'll speak to you soon." I hung up and cradled Pete in my arms, awkwardly holding him while we knelt on the floor of the cab, wrapped in woollen blankets in forty-degree heat. Sweat poured off me, as it did Pete, but we still held on. He sucked in a breath and blew it out slowly, calming himself down and peeling himself away. He pulled back so he could look in my eyes.

Cupping my face, touching me as if he were making sure I was real, he stuttered, "I... you... Scottie..." before his face crumpled and his tears began again.

"Shh, it's okay. I'm here." I pulled him close again, rocking him gently until the door was yanked open, and Waru stood there, reaching for us and patting us down. Checking us.

His voice wavered, full of fear and regret. "Scottie, Macca," he breathed, tears choking him up. He cleared his throat and started again. "You blokes all right?"

"Yeah, mate," I croaked, nodding. His reaction diffused my fury a little but didn't dissipate it altogether. "What the fuck happened? Why'd you leave him?"

"I didn't. I swear, mate. The bull trapped itself in the fence. I had to cut it away and repair the fence. I dunno why it was even out there. Stupid bloody thing. Then I looked up and the fire was right there. I've been driving since, ran straight through two fences to get here, but I didn't make it." He sobbed and reached out for Pete, grasping his shoulder. "I'm so sorry."

"You okay? Injured at all?"

"No." He shook his head.

"Let's get back to the homestead then." I couldn't say more. My nerves were fried, my emotions raw. I know he'd done what he could, but his everything wasn't good enough. Pete wouldn't have made it if I'd left it up to Waru. And for that, I wasn't sure I could ever forgive him.

"Yeah, boss." He nodded sadly and closed the door.

I ran my fingers through Pete's hair. "You okay?" He nodded, and I dropped a kiss to his head, silently thanking the spirits of the land for getting me there in time. For giving me the chance to save him. The words were on the tip of my tongue, a declaration of love. Eight letters. Three words. I'd never uttered them to another human being who didn't share my blood. But I had no doubt that it was real with Pete.

"Scottie, take me home?" he whispered, his voice breaking as he sniffed again.

"Yeah." I nodded and pressed another kiss to his forehead before helping him climb over the front seat. I wasn't ready yet to let him go, and I didn't think he was either. I clambered ungracefully into the front, never letting go of Pete's hand, and slid into my seat. Pete leaned over the centre console, getting as close as he possibly could, and holding onto my arm like a lifeline. I squeezed his fingers and turned the ignition a click. It sputtered and all the warning lights lit the dash. Beeps and flashing lights had me holding my breath, concern pulsing through me while I turned it over. It groaned, the engine whining before it started. I blew out a relieved breath and made the journey back to the homestead a lot slower. I'd probably cracked the suspension, and even though the fire probably hadn't touched the car directly, it had likely fried half the electronics in the car, but I didn't care. He was alive and unharmed.

I pulled up at the front of the homestead and opened Pete's door for him, holding his hand as he stepped out. As soon as he was standing, I pulled him into my arms and kissed him. Wrapped up in my arms, one hand at his nape, I pulled Pete's face down to mine and kissed him, pouring all my frayed emotions into our touch. We broke apart, each sucking in a breath, and I whispered the words I'd needed to say for an age against his lips. "I love you."

Pete stilled and then smiled, his grin reflecting pure happiness. "I love you, too."

I let my eyes drift closed and pulled him closer as the adrenaline finally began to subside. I shook, trembling in his arms as I breathed him in, kissing his throat as we clung to each other.

When I finally managed to pry myself away from Pete, I brushed another kiss over his lips and said, "Come inside." He nodded, his eyes still closed, and I took his hand in mine, turning to walk up the steps. Ma and Nan were standing there, holding onto each other, Jono wrapping a protective arm around Ma as tears streamed down her face. Ally stood with Sam, his arms around her as she wiped her face. Waru and Yindi stood to the side, Yindi touching Waru in the same way that I'd checked Pete over. Den was there too, standing closest to us and right next to Craig. I stopped short. Seeing everyone's eyes on me made me stutter, my steps halting before they'd even begun. I shifted Pete protectively behind me and stood there, waiting for the wrath of my station hands.

"Seriously? We're not gonna say anything?" Craig huffed. "Look, I'm as glad as anyone that you're back, but mate, you're a poofter?"

His derision was a slap to my face, stealing my words and my breath. I opened my mouth, gaping. I knew it'd be like this, but the reality of it was a gut punch. I didn't even realize I'd let go of Pete's hand until he pushed past me and ran for the guest house. My feet were rooted to the spot, watching in slow motion as my world unravelled itself. Pete was running away from me. A rushing sounded in my ears, and it was as if I was detached from my own body. Looking down on myself. I willed my legs to move, to go after him, but I was stuck. Unable to get the message from my brain to my limbs. But in that split second, I looked around. Watching Pete's retreating form and those people who I'd called family. I tried speaking again, my mouth opening, but nothing came forth. Then I turned my gaze inwards and really looked at myself. Summoned up every scathing remark I'd heard and cast them aside. I couldn't love Pete until I could accept myself. And in that moment, I realized I didn't care what Craig or anyone else said. I accepted me. I was gay.

Jono stepped forward, gripping my biceps. "Son, listen to me." He shook me once, trying to snap me out of my own thoughts. "You're the best station manager I know. I respect the hell outta you. I don't care who you love. As long as you treat everyone right and the animals well, you've got my respect. But that right there?" He pointed to the guesthouse. "That wasn't treating your boy right. Go to him and be the boyfriend he needs." I nodded at him, his words slowly sinking in, but he didn't let go. Instead, he turned to everyone else and spoke, his tone brooking no argument. "Anyone else here have a problem with Scottie and Pete, and you can fuck right off. Sorry, Ma, Lynn." Jono squeezed my shoulder and spoke to me again. "Go."

With that one word, I snapped back into myself, time catching up and my legs being released from the hold they'd been under. I ran, sprinted across the yard, over the red dirt and dry patchy grass. Up the steps to the veranda and grasped the doorknob. I probably looked like some deranged creature, wild-eyed with a heaving chest, crashing through the door. I needed to tell him. I needed to show him what was in my heart.

But then I saw him. Sitting on the end of the bed, his elbows resting on his knees, his head hung low. He was breathing deep, long, slow breaths. I skidded to a stop, falling to my knees in front of him. I grasped each of his knees, but Pete pulled away.

"Scottie, I can't—"

I pressed my fingers to his lips, desperately trying to stop the words from falling past his lips and reached for him again. "Wait. Listen. Please." I took a breath and my words fell out of my lips in a rush. "I love you. I don't want to hide anymore. I'm gay and I'm proud of that. Proud to be with you. I'm glad I'm out. That they all know. That fire…. God." I shook my head and closed my eyes, warding off the horror show of what could have happened if I didn't make it to him in time. "I just want to love you. That's it. I don't care about anything else or anyone's opinions. It doesn't matter. *They* don't matter. You do, and I do too. I love you. You're the most important thing to me. You. No more hiding. No more pretending. I want to walk out of here holding your hand. I want to be able to kiss you and hold you. I want to give you everything you've ever dreamed of. I want you to move in with me properly. I want to grow old with you."

Tears shined in Pete's red-rimmed eyes. His face was dirty from soot and smoke, tear tracks smeared on his cheeks. Even under the dirt, I could see how pale his skin was. Even his freckles were ghostly white. His hair was matted, messy. It looked like he'd gone through hell and back.

But the light that sparked in his green eyes at my words gave me hope. "You do?"

"I do." I nodded. He tugged me to him and pulled me into his arms, holding me tight.

"Can we move my stuff now?" he mumbled into my shoulder. "I don't want to waste another moment."

I laughed, happiness bursting in my chest, and I squeezed him tighter, nodding. "Yes." So, we did exactly that. I grabbed his duffel bag, stuffing the two remaining tees he had in the drawers into it, while Pete slipped his laptop into its cover and placed the paperwork that littered the small table into a box, stacking both up ready to go. I handed him the mostly empty duffel and took the heavier paperwork before opening the door for him. Holding his hand proudly, I brushed a kiss to his knuckles and let the door bang closed behind me.

No one stood at the steps to the main house anymore, but we could hear voices coming from the long table in the dining room. Conversation ceased once we stepped through the door, and I scanned the faces there. Sam had his arm around Ally, and she'd turned into him. Jono's and Craig's places were empty. "Where are they?" I asked, my voice wavering as I pointed to Jono's chair. After his words, surely he wouldn't leave. Would he?

"Craig wanted out, so Jono's driving him to Longreach," Sam said. "The rest of us…." He shook his head. "Scottie, it makes no bit of difference to any of us who you love. And Macca, you're a good bloke." Sam shrugged. "We're happy for you." Ally nodded in agreement, but she'd been crying too.

"Thanks, mate. I appreciate you sayin' that. But if you'll excuse us, Pete's just agreed to move in with me."

Nan rose and wrapped me in her thin arms. "I'm proud as hell of you, Scottie." She reached out for Pete, pulling him close too. "Make sure you treat each other right."

"We will, Nan," Pete responded, squeezing my hand. She let us go, and we made a move to my bedroom, but I stopped and smiled at the people gathered around, supporting us. My family.

FOURTEEN

Pete

Scottie and I held hands as we pulled into the co-op in Longreach two days after the fire. I'd been dehydrated and copped a bit of heat exhaustion from it, spending the day in bed, drinking water, and sleeping off the headache and muscle cramps. Scottie refused to leave my side and sent the others out to assess the damage to the property.

They'd come back reporting that there was a hell of a lot of work to be done. Wide tracts of fences had been burned, many of the timber posts charred up and needing replacement. We'd made the trip into Longreach to order supplies to fix the fences and for a doctor's check-up. While we were sitting in the, waiting room, an older couple had walked in and greeted Scottie with the warmth of old friends, the lady hugging him and the man shaking his hand and squeezing his shoulder. He'd introduced me then to his neighbours and I understood exactly why they'd treated him like family. Then Mary dropped a bombshell, shocking Scottie when she told him that if he hadn't called the doc out to see them, she'd be blind. Apparently, her condition was treatable, and she'd had surgery to fix the problem and was healing well.

Once the doc confirmed I was okay, we headed over to the co-op to order supplies. We met Bob, the owner, at the front counter. "G'day, mate," Scottie greeted.

"Scottie," he replied curtly.

Scottie ignored his tone, but his eyes hardened. "This is Pete McKenzie."

"The boyfriend, I've heard." He sneered and added, "We don't want your kind here."

Scottie laughed. "My kind? You've been serving me for years, Bob, and never had a problem taking my money before. But you know what, that's cool. I'll go take my business to your competition."

We walked out and Scottie strode around to the driver side, closing the door behind him as if nothing was wrong. "Wait, that's it? You're not going to do anything about him?"

"Nope. I spend shitloads of money there. I'll let my wallet talk." He dialled a number and the ringing came through the speakers of the Landcruiser.

"Hello?" Nan answered.

"Hi, Nan. It's me. Bob at the co-op apparently doesn't like my kind. I'm guessin' Craig's been mouthing off. Can you please have Ma close our account there. Anything that's outstanding that we can cancel, pull it. I'm going across town. If they have the same attitude, I'll order from Charleville, or hell, the Isa or Emerald if I have to." She assured him it'd be done, and when he hung up, I reached for him.

"I'm sorry. This is exactly what you were afraid of."

"Don't apologize," he said, brushing his thumb over my knuckles. "I don't care if I have to drive to bloody Melbourne to get supplies. If they have a problem with us, it's their problem, not ours. When Craig called me a poof, it made me realize that I don't care anymore what anyone thinks. I'm me, and if anyone can't accept that I'm gay, then bugger 'em." He kissed me then, a slow press of his lips against my knuckles, right there in the car park of the co-op in the main street of Longreach for anyone to see. And I couldn't help but swoon a little and grin a lot.

We drove across town to the other supplier and walked in, hand in hand. Scottie was making a statement. It was a giant "fuck you" to anyone who didn't like it. Probably not the smartest idea in an outback town where things could turn ugly for us real quick, but I was proud of Scottie for standing up for himself. We went straight to the counter, a woman with grey hair and ruddy red cheeks greeting us. "What can I do for you gents today?" she asked with a smile.

"I'd like to set up an account, please," Scottie said, handing over his licence. Her eyes widened momentarily, and she looked up again. "Scott Pearce from Pearce Station?"

"That's me." He nodded. "And this is my partner, Pete McKenzie."

"Nice to meet you both. I'm Nell." She came around the counter and shook hands with us. "Come into my office and we can get the paperwork started. "Daz, you've got the counter," she called out.

"No worries, Ma," a voice answered.

"I know you've been Bob's client for years. Why the change if you don't mind me asking?" she queried when we sat down.

"Bob apparently doesn't like our kind," Scottie huffed, rolling his eyes. "So bugger him. I'll take my business where it's welcome. Is it welcome here?"

"Absolutely, Mr Pearce. Bloody narrow-minded fool. Does he think you're the only gay man in the outback?" She shook her head. "You won't find shitty attitudes here, Mr Pearce, only good service."

"Scottie, please. And thank you."

We spent a good hour there, sorting everything out and ordering enough fencing supplies to do the repairs. When we'd finished, Nell shook our hands again. "Good doing business, gents. Let us know if you need anything else."

"We will. We have a few large projects coming up that we'll be getting started on soon."

We made our way to the pub for lunch. By silent agreement, we went straight to the same one we'd reconnected at. The historic building was welcoming, filled with dark timber panelling and the smell of malt and yeast. We ordered lunch and sat down, each of us nursing a beer. "Incoming," I muttered to Scottie, seeing Craig of all people approaching us.

"Craig," Scottie greeted with a nod.

"Mate, I need to apologize," he started. "Can I interrupt you?" His shoulders sagged when Scottie raised an eyebrow at him. Finally, Scottie motioned to one of the empty chairs and Craig slumped into it, putting his beer down on the table.

"What brings on the change of heart?"

"I walked away from Ally and Sam. They're my best friends and I walked away because I was stupid. I broke us apart. It was a knee-jerk reaction. I was shocked and I didn't think. When Sam chose to stay with Ally over leaving with me, I realized I'd made a mistake. My pride got in the way and—" He shrugged, shaking his head. "—I had to follow through. Jono drove me here and for four hours didn't say a single word. When I said bye, he told me he was disappointed in me. I went to the co-op to let Bob know I needed work if anyone was looking. He asked me why I was leavin', and I told him it's because you're gay." He huffed and rubbed his eyes with the heel of his hands. "Saying it now sounds as ridiculous as it did when I told Bob, but the way he reacted... I don't think I've seen anyone so disgusted, and I was ashamed of myself for acting exactly the same way. I didn't ask if you were okay—you'd just been in a bloody fire for God's sake. You're good to us, Scottie. You're a good bloke. You didn't deserve the way I treated you. Nor you, Macca. So, I'm sorry."

Scottie sighed and closed his eyes. "I won't stand for any disrespect, Craig. One snide comment, one smart-arse remark and you're out. But I appreciate your apology. If you wanna come home, we'd be happy to have you back."

"Seriously?" he asked, wide-eyed. "Because yeah, that'd be bonza."

I couldn't help my snort of laughter. I don't think I'd ever heard anyone say "bonza." It was one of those Aussie idioms from the days of *Crocodile Dundee* that just didn't get said anymore. Scottie kicked me under the table, and I laughed harder. Soon we were clinking glasses and drinking to Craig's return.

We got up after another hour or so, all three of us swapping to Coke after our one and only round of beers. Scottie clapped Craig on the shoulder as we walked out.

The three of us walked out of the pub, Craig heading to the motel to get his things and us to the Landcruiser parked on the street. We had a welcoming party when we got there. Bob and someone he obviously knew were leaning against the four-by-four. I ground my teeth together seeing their disrespect. "Bob," Scottie grated. "Mind movin' off my truck?"

"You had the cheek to pull your account from me?" he seethed.

"You were the one who said you won't serve my kind, Bob." Scottie shrugged, playing it off casually, but I could read him well enough to see his tells. His fisted hands, his short sharp breaths, his voice sounding slightly choked.

Bob didn't like his answer. He strode forward, getting in Scottie's personal space. Scottie didn't break eye contact with him but subtly shifted to cover me with his body.

Craig charged down the footpath towards the two men standing chest to chest and dropped his rucksack at our feet. "What are you doin', dickhead?" Craig swore, shoving in front of Scottie and pushing Bob back. "Back off, mate."

We were in a bloody three-way standoff. It was exactly what Scottie had feared by coming out. That his suppliers would turn. His clients would run. That he wouldn't be able to walk into Longreach without constantly looking over his shoulder. It was a matter of safety now too. And we were gathering an audience.

"Scottie, Craig, Bob, everything okay?" Frank said.

"Scottie here thinks he's top shit now that he's a faggot." Bob spat at the ground, the glob of spittle landing close to Scottie's booted foot on the concrete footpath. "Too good to shop at the co-op now."

Frank looked him over. Looked at Bob's mate, who wore the same disgusted scowl that Bob did. Looked at Craig, chest heaving, and nostrils flaring as he stood in front of Scottie with a hand held out to Bob, stopping him from moving forward. Scottie, who still had a hand on me, pushing me behind him. "You can close my account too, Bob. I won't have you disrespecting my friends."

"Go back to the co-op, mate," Craig added quietly. "You don't want to make this more than it is."

Bob seemed to regain his senses and shook his head, disgust pouring off him in waves. "You're as bad as him. You buddying up with the gays now 'cause it's the done thing, huh? PC bullshit. You ain't welcome in my shop. None of you." He pointed to Scottie and to Frank, then spun on his heels and left. His mate glared at us, shooting daggers, before he followed Bob, slinking back towards the co-op on foot.

Scottie blew out a breath and laid a hand on Craig's shoulder. "Thanks, mate. I appreciate you stepping in." Craig nodded at Scottie, then turned to Frank and Mary. He tipped his hat. "Mrs Harrison, Frank."

"Frank, that wasn't necessary. You shouldn't have compromised your relationship with Bob, but thank you. I appreciate the sentiment." Scottie held out his hand to Frank and he shook it, their grips firm.

"That's what friends do, Scottie." Frank still held Scottie's hand and with his other, rested it on Scottie's shoulder. "You dropped everything when you knew we needed help. You were there for us. You saved Mary's sight by getting the doc out there. You fixed our bore, so the animals had water, and you brought us food and feed. It's the least I could do."

"Is it true?" Mary asked, a small smile on her face. Scottie went rigid next to me. "I'm guessing that Macca, here, is your partner?"

"I am." I stepped forward, resting my hand on Scottie's lower back.

"And it was you who talked Scottie into applying for the government grant? We couldn't have applied for it either without his help, and it's saved our station." She reached out, patting my forearm. "Thank you."

"It was my pleasure." I smiled at her and turned to Scottie, who grinned right back at me.

That night, back at the station, we all ended up around the kitchen table, playing poker. Scottie's family surrounded us, and now mine. It was warmth and acceptance. So different from our run-in with Bob. But Frank's acceptance of Scottie had meant the world. He was an old-timer, someone who Scottie probably assumed would be as dead against us as Bob was. But Frank's words made Scottie hold his head up high. Embrace the man right there in the street and do the same to his lovely wife.

There was laughter all round, affectionate and playful ribbing. Happiness. "So," Sam started, "You met your in-laws yet, Scottie?"

"Um...."

"How about now?" I asked, looking at the time. It wasn't late—only a little after nine. Mum and Dad would still be awake and it'd been weeks since I'd spoken to them, even though I'd been emailing them regularly. Scottie looked at me wide-eyed, a little panicked, and I grinned at him, grabbing his hand. "Come on, let me brag to someone about you for once."

We made our way into Scottie's bedroom—our bedroom now—slower than I'd ever seen him walk before, and I sat on the end of the bed while I loaded up messenger on my laptop. "It's okay. We can just call rather than video chatting," he muttered, hesitating near the doorway.

"Scott Pearce, sit your arse down." I laughed, reaching out to him. "They don't bite."

Mum picked up her phone after a few rings. She was sitting on the couch, their kitchen table behind her decorated with a bunch of vibrant flowers in a crystal vase. Her hair sat loosely around her face, and she was wearing a pink and white pin-striped shirt. With a smile, she waved. "Hi, honey, how are you?" Another voice in the background—my dad— added, "Pete, good to hear from you."

We chatted briefly and I pulled Scottie closer. "Mum, Dad, I'd like to introduce you to… my guy. Scottie, meet my mum and dad. Mum, Dad, this is Scottie."

They were shocked silent. Mum's mouth hung open and Dad wore a stunned expression. "I thought you were doing research somewhere out near Longreach?" Dad blurted, and I laughed.

"Yeah, I am, but there's more to it than what I've told you too." Mum's brow furrowed and her lips straightened, thinning out. I continued, giving them the full story. "You're always at me to do something productive with my time, rather than wasting it chasing Byron's gold—"

"Peter," Dad warned.

"Dad let me finish," I cried, my frustration showing through. I carried the laptop with me, reaching into the top drawer on the side of the bed Scottie had cleared out for me, my fingers closing around the cannister. "Well, I was getting nowhere. But then I had a breakthrough. My research led me to Pearce Station, south-west of Longreach, like I told you. But I'm not writing a paper like you thought I was. I've been prospecting for Byron's gold. Scottie runs Pearce Station with his family."

"So, you chased a myth halfway across the country, and what, you two hit it off?" Mum asked, her eyes wide, eyebrows hiked up, and a small smile on her face.

I thought about her summary and shrugged. "Yeah, in a nutshell, and I've figured out what I want to do. I'm staying here. Moving here permanently."

"Okay...." Dad answered. "So you're done with chasing that ridiculous myth? You're going to settle down?"

"Not quite," I answered, holding up the clear plastic container filled with gold. "This is just part of it. One morning's prospecting."

"Is that...?" Mum asked.

"It is." I nodded. "I think I've found the reef, but even if I haven't, it doesn't matter." I looked across to Scottie and smiled at him, linking my fingers with his. "I've found where I'm meant to be."

Mum and Dad told us how happy they were for us, and Dad congratulated me for going with my gut, rather than listening to him. Scottie squeezed my hand and I leaned into him, smiling the whole time. They talked to Scottie, asking him questions about the station, about him, Ma, Nan, and Ally too, and by the time they'd changed the subject to Mum and Dad visiting, or our travelling to Sydney to see them, Scottie had charmed Mum completely. When he mentioned taking them for a horse ride, Dad perked up, asking all about breeds and pedigree. By the time we'd hung up, Scottie had invited them to stay in the guesthouse, explaining that now I'd moved in with him, it'd be free. I'd grinned happily and leaned into him and Scottie hadn't hesitated, wrapping his arm around me and kissing my temple with a smile on his lips.

I ended the call and closed my laptop lid, sliding it off the bed to the floor. Crawling into his lap, I murmured, "I love you," against his lips and smiled when he leaned into me, chasing my lips.

Scottie picked up the gold I'd discovered and smiled. "You found Byron's treasure."

I basked in his strong arms surrounding me. His protectiveness. He'd been worried about calling, about asking me to come back from my expedition to the reef. He'd thought he was being possessive, and I wouldn't appreciate it. Then he'd rescued me, saved me from a threat I hadn't even realized was there until it was too late to protect myself. Without him, it was unlikely I would have made it to safety. I'd been on my last legs. I'd left it too long to get water and was tired, thirsty, and overheated already. When I'd smelt smoke, the fire was already on top of me. The walls of the gully had stopped the smoke reaching down into the area I'd been in until the ravine itself was on fire.

It wasn't the first time he'd saved me either.

I wasn't some damsel in distress, but I was sure as hell grateful for him rescuing me. He gave me so much of himself. The little things—the secret smiles, holding me at night, trusting me with his heart. And I loved every part of him. I traced my fingertips down his jawline, his stubble soft against my fingers. I carded my fingers through his hair and ran my nose down his. When his eyes met mine, I gazed into his blue eyes, the same colour as the outback sky, that sparked with a warmth that wrapped around me and travelled right down to my bones. He was beautiful, inside and out. I pressed my lips to his and kissed him slowly.

"No," I whispered, plucking the cannister of precious metal from his fingers and tossing it aside. "I found *my* treasure."

Epilogue

A year later

I sat on the swing hanging from the rafters on the homestead's veranda. Pete was in my arms, one foot hooked over the armrest, the other swinging us slowly. Steam curled over the lip of my mug, and I brought it to my mouth, blowing it away as I took a sip. Pete had a coffee in his hand, his mug already half-finished. We were watching the world go by after having spent days preparing the station. High winds and strong rains were predicted, but having seen no rain for years, none of us were holding our breaths.

Some big changes had happened on the station in the last twelve months. The gold bands we wore, prospected from our very own land, attested to that. We weren't married. But we had made a commitment to each other. We'd found the gold together, prospecting side by side. Pete had joked about smelting down the pieces he'd found and wearing them around his neck, and it'd planted a seed, both of us wanting to wear our connection with each other and the land we were the caretakers of. The jeweller in Longreach had designed us a simple band, and Pete suggested we decorate it with an engraving of the horizon line from the station. We'd stolen out at night on horseback, camping out under the southern cross sky—a blanket of a billion stars and the full moon as our witnesses—and we'd exchanged them, promising to love each other for all time.

Pete and I were happy. Deliriously so. We lived and worked together. The red dirt of the outback ran in our veins. It was part of us. The clear blue sky, a comfort. Home. This lifestyle wasn't for everyone. Ma and Dad's failed relationship had left me jaded. I'd resigned myself to a lifetime of being alone, save for hook-ups when I was in the big cities. I'd never dreamed that a gorgeous redhead would pull up and flirt with me over a bonfire, then clamber into my lap at the mention of a snake. He'd shaken up my staid and monochrome world and allowed me to see the future for what it was. Full of beauty and life and love. He'd given me the courage to unapologetically be me, and he loved me for it. He'd changed my future in an instant, and I adored him for it.

Pete travelling here wasn't just luck. This land, the spirits, worked in mysterious ways. They knew I would be stronger with him by my side. They gave me the one man who loved this land as much as me. He'd told me that he was drawn here. That he'd been captivated by Byron's story the first time he'd heard it. It had taken him years of learning, of research and wading through history—both fact and fiction—to be ready to find this place. To find me. He'd said that when he first turned onto the property and saw our Pearce Station sign hanging from the timber post near our rusted letterbox, he'd felt like he was coming home. It was as if the land was welcoming him.

And he'd stayed. My fear that one day he'd wake up and realize what he was missing was gone. It no longer held any power over me. He'd shown me over and over again how hard he loved. But it wasn't only love for me that made him stay. He wasn't trapped like my father had felt. No, Pete truly had found his way home.

We weren't the only changes happening, though. Something had shifted between Jono and Ma too. They'd been dancing around each other for decades, but they'd finally taken a close look at themselves. We'd now see them holding hands or smiling softly at each other over a cuppa in the afternoons, and I was elated for them. Ma deserved someone who treated her like a queen, and Jono did exactly that. I was thrilled to see that the man, who was more of a dad than my own had ever been, happy and finally able to show how much he loved her. There were no two people more destined to be together than they were.

Angry clouds rolled over the horizon in the distance, lightning flashing across the sky in jagged lines. Thunder followed long seconds later. Heat had ratcheted up, but the storm was still too far away from us to have any effect. We were playing a waiting game, begging the spirits of the land to help it reach us. Hoping against hope for rain. We'd had long, hard years since it'd last rained, the drought ravaging us and the land we lived on. The gold had helped immeasurably—we were thriving financially despite being totally reliant on feed and potable water being trucked in. We'd buckled down, doing even more to restrict the amount we used to try and conserve our natural resources, but it was hard. And we were tired.

Time ticked by and I kept my gaze riveted to the clouds. I took Pete's empty mug and set it down beside mine as the others joined us, watching the storm track closer and closer. It moved slowly, the lightning and thunder ramping up. We'd experienced so much heartache as a nation in the last couple of years. Drought, floods, cyclones, and bushfires that had scorched the earth, killing hundreds of millions of animals, destroying livelihoods, and killing far too many people. We'd watched the news in horror as the nation's koala population was brought to its knees, after already suffering from the spread of disease, and dehydration from the drought. So many of those fires had been started by lightning, their intensity magnified by the extreme dry brought on by the drought and the reduction in the window of opportunity to conduct preventative burning safely. Climate change was to blame, but our pollies in Canberra were still ignoring the issue.

The dry lightning was what worried me with this storm. If we didn't get the rain that accompanied the lightning, it could be disastrous. We'd already lost so much of our remnant vegetation from the last grassfire. That had been caused by a cigarette butt, but regardless of the cause, burning of any of the remaining areas would be catastrophic for our native animals.

Tens of thousands of hectares had burned in the last fire. We'd been relatively lucky, the fire skirting the edge of our property and only killing one bull—the one Waru had cut loose—but we'd found countless kangaroos, wombats, echidnas, and dingoes dead too. It'd inspired us all to ramp up our efforts to create a wildlife sanctuary on our property. To return some of the land to them. We'd worked towards closing down one of our largest paddocks, allowing the land to recuperate and become a safe haven. Waru and Yindi's people had helped us, making sure we were doing things right, and we'd ceremoniously erected a sign at the entrance to the paddock, declaring it closed for cattle. And the bore troughs we'd erected were working. The footage from motion sensor cameras we'd mounted near them showed every kind of wildlife using them. It was as if they were entering neutral territory, temporarily declaring a truce between predator and prey for the chance to drink.

Now we were just waiting for rain.

To regenerate the land. To cleanse us from drought.

The cooling wind reached us first. My heart rate notched up and hope bloomed in my chest. Pete squeezed my hand as he felt it too. Would the rains come? The storm was so close that we could almost reach out and touch the clouds. They sat heavy in the air, dark and ominous to the inexperienced. To us, they brought life. Hope. The metallic grey-blue of the clouds made even the most hardened of outback folk take a moment to thank mother nature for her greatest gift to us.

I breathed deep, the smell of damp soil, the freshness of the rains washing away the dust permeating my senses. My breath caught in my throat and Pete smiled at me, his gaze full of hope. Anticipation. Love. The first drops on our corrugated iron roof was the sweetest of music to my ears, and my tears fell freely. It'd been years since I'd heard that sound. Years since a single drop of rain had fallen on our lands. The drops sped up as the rain washed over us, beginning in earnest. I lifted my face to the sky and listened, not a single person speaking as we took it in. Pete tugged on my hand, pulling me up. He dragged me off the steps and into the rain, laughing as the cool drops kissed our skin. He tore off my old Akubra and tossed it aside, his own hat following, and we tilted our faces up to the sky. The rain fell, and I held my arms out wide, whooping in glee. I was grateful for every drop that touched me. That touched our land. We were blessed. Now we had it all. My tears of sweet relief mixed with the water running in rivulets down my face, and Pete was there in my arms, laugh-crying too. He was tugging my tee off my body, pulling it over my head and stripping his off too. Puddles formed around us, the rain falling in sheets as I looked up at my man. At my lover. My best friend and soulmate. Our spirits soared, dancing and twirling gracefully together in the rain like ballerinas.

I kissed him, my eyes falling closed as I wrapped my arms around him tight and pressed our bodies together. All the while, we got wetter. Fat drops fell, and we laughed and kissed, our bodies swaying to music only we could hear.

Whoops and hollers sounded from around us, and I watched as our family got in on our crazy. T-shirts and boots got stripped off, mud and water being kicked up as they laughed and danced in the rain. Always together, always strong. Pearce Station was my home. This land forever a part of me. I'd gained Pete in this last year. He'd become part of me too, sharing his heart with me and never letting go.

Rain was the sign of hope. The sign of new beginnings and easier times ahead. I wasn't sure what the future held for us, but I knew down to my bones that whatever we faced, we'd do it together, with our family by our sides. I looked around, my gaze connecting with them. Ma and Jono, who had their arms interlinked, spinning and splashing, Nan slow dancing with Den, Ally with her arms wrapped around the two men who never left her side, Waru and Yindi swaying together, all of them surrounding Pete and me. Happiness settled in my bones, my future laid out before me with this beautiful man by my side. I'd fallen in love with the boy from the city and uncovered a treasure worth far more than all the gold in these lands. And like the gold, and the red dirt and the blue sky, we'd endure. Our futures interlinked forever with each other and with the land we called home.

The end

ABOUT ANN GRECH

By day Ann Grech lives in the corporate world and can be found sitting behind a desk typing away at reports and papers or lecturing to a room full of students. She graduated with a PhD in 2016 and is now an over-qualified nerd. Glasses, briefcase, high heels and a pencil skirt, she's got the librarian look nailed too. If only they knew! She swears like a sailor, so that's got to be a hint. The other one was "the look" from her tattoo artist when she told him that she wanted her kids initials "B" and "J" tattooed on her foot. It took a second to register that it might be a bad idea.

She's never entirely fit in and loves escaping into a book—whether it's reading or writing one. But she's found her tribe now and loves her MM book world family. She dislikes cooking, but loves eating, can't figure out technology, but is addicted to it, and her guilty pleasure is Byron Bay Cookies. Oh and shoes. And lingerie. And maybe handbags too. Well, if we're being honest, we'd probably have to add her library too given the state of her credit card every month (what can she say, she's a bookworm at heart)!

She also publishes her raunchier short stories under her pen name, Olive Hiscock.

Ann loves chatting to people online, so if you'd like to keep up with what she's got going on:

Join her newsletter: http://anngrech.us8.list-manage2.com/subscribe?u=0af7475c0791ed8f1466e7fd9&id=1cee9cdcb6

Like her on Facebook: https://www.facebook.com/pages/Ann-Grech/458420227655212

Join her reader group: https://www.facebook.com/groups/1871698189780535/

Follow her on Twitter and Instagram: @anngrechauthor

Follow her on Goodreads: https://www.goodreads.com/author/show/7536397.Ann_Grech

Follow her on BookBub: https://www.bookbub.com/authors/ann-grech

Visit her website (www.anngrech.com) for her current booklist

She'd love to hear from you directly, too. Please feel free to e-mail her at ann@anngrech.com or check out her website www.anngrech.com for updates.

Other books by Ann Grech

UNEXPECTED

Whiteout (MM)
White Noise (MM)
Whitewash (MM)

MY TRUTH

All He Needs (MMM)
In Safe Arms (MM)

GOLD COAST NIGHTS

Delectable (MMF)

MV DREAMCATCHER

Dance with Me (MM)

STANDALONES

Home For Christmas (MM)
The Gift (FMMM - free for newsletter subscribers)

M/F TITLES

One night in Daytona
Ink'd